LOVE'S BITTER MEMORIES

Brooke Hildreth was young, beautiful and wealthy. She had everything any woman could want, but then she became a widow one hour after her marriage to the man she loved . . . Trying to escape from her unhappy past and the dark secret buried in her heart, Brooke sought peace and solitude in her uncle's mountain home. When two men interrupted that quiet, Brooke found herself faced with love again — but could her tortured heart accept it?

Books by Peggy Gaddis
in the Linford Romance Library:

NURSE'S CHOICE
EVERGLADES NURSE
CAROLINA LOVE SONG
NURSE AT THE CEDARS
A NURSE CALLED HAPPY
NURSE ANGELA
NURSE AT SPANISH CAY
THE NURSE WAS JULIET
LUXURY NURSE
NURSE IN THE SHADOWS
LEOTA FOREMAN, RN

PEGGY GADDIS

LOVE'S BITTER MEMORIES

Complete and Unabridged

LINFORD
Leicester

First published in the
United States of America

Original title 'Peacock Hill'

First Linford Edition
published January 1994

British Library CIP Data

Gaddis, Peggy
    Love's bitter memories.—Large print ed.—
Linford romance library
    I. Title II. Series
    813.52 [F]

    ISBN 0–7089–7507–0

Published by
F. A. Thorpe (Publishing) Ltd.
Anstey, Leicestershire

Set by Words & Graphics Ltd.
Anstey, Leicestershire
Printed and bound in Great Britain by
T. J. Press (Padstow) Ltd., Padstow, Cornwall

This book is printed on acid-free paper

1

THE storm hurled itself against the old log house with a fury that was demoniac. But the old house, which had weathered more than a hundred years of such storms, stood sturdily, as though contemptuous of such fury. Leafless trees were twisted and tortured by the wind; a deluge of cold rain hurled itself at the windows through which yellow lamplight spilled out into the darkness.

Inside the big main room of the house, Robin and her brother Kirke ignored the storm as casually as the house did. Rose-colored curtains of a rough mountain weave had been drawn across the windows, allowing only rosy shadows to be seen.

A huge open fireplace welcomed four foot logs, blazing cheerily; firelight fell on rustic, sturdy furniture made by mountain craftsmen to last as long as the house. The final note of cheer against the night's storm was the big gray cat, curled on the old rag rug in front of the fire, her five kittens tumbling about her happily.

Robin sat curled in a big old chair, her legs drawn up under her. She wore a flannel shirt, blue jeans and battered scuffs on her feet. Her black hair, cut short, frothed over her head in a cap of curls, and her book lay neglected on her knees. On the other side of the table that held the lamp, Kirke sprawled contentedly, absorbed in the newspaper that had come with the day's mail.

Robin said softly, her blue eyes on the cat, "Sometimes I envy Samanthy."

Kirke looked up, puzzled, a grin dancing on his lean brown face.

"Because she has five babies to look after?" he asked politely.

Robin chuckled. "No, because she can purr when she's happy. I can't. She's as happy to be home as I am.

But she can prove it by purring, and I can't."

Kirke put down his paper. Now the grin had vanished from his face and his eyes, as blue as hers, were warm.

"Was it so bad in the valley at Aunt Zelda's?" he asked gently.

"Oh, of course not," Robin answered hastily. "And besides, I had to get an education, didn't I, and learn to look after you when you came home? It wasn't bad at all. It was just — well, after all, I hate valleys and I love the mountains."

Kirke nodded thoughtfully and reached for his pipe and filled it.

"I know, honey. Many's the time in Saudi Arabia when I looked at the impressive wages I was receiving and wondered if it was worth it, to put in so much time out there where it was hot." He broke off, grinned and went on briskly, "But it *did* give us a nice bank roll, so we could buy a home power plant and have electricity and

3

running water and all the comforts of civilization."

"Oh, sure," Robin answered. Kirke sat erect, frowning.

"What was that?" he asked sharply.

"What was what?" Robin asked.

"That noise?"

Robin eyed him amusedly.

"Old Man Winter roaring his head off because he knows he'll have to check out soon and make way for spring."

"No, listen — "

Kirke was on his feet now, hurrying to the big door. A huddled heap lay against the door, and as he opened it, the heap fell into the room.

"Robin, it's somebody caught in the storm — " Kirke was bending above the huddle, and as he lifted it in his arms, he added, shocked, "Why, it's a woman!"

As he lifted her, a fur coat sodden with rain slid from her shoulders and fell with a little wet 'plop' on the floor, and he kicked it out of his way as he

4

hurried toward the big chair Robin had drawn close to the fire.

He put the woman very gently into the chair, looked down at her anxiously and said swiftly, "Get those wet clothes off her, Robin. Bundle her in a blanket while I get some coffee. She's wet to the skin."

He hurried out, and Robin, her blue eyes very wide, began swiftly to strip off the woman's sodden garments. When Kirke came back, Robin had put the woman into one of her own flannelette nightgowns and had bundled her into a thick blanket.

The coffee was steaming hot, and as Robin tried to feed it to the woman, careful spoonful by spoonful, Kirke knelt on the hearth rug and with a big rough towel began drying her feet, from which Robin had removed remnants of breath-thin nylons and high-heeled, sharp-toed patent-leather pumps.

Robin brought a towel and began drying the woman's hair. The firelight twinkled on its thick, curling masses, and Robin, faintly awed, said, "Why, Kirke, her hair is just the color of a new penny!"

Gradually the woman stirred as the warmth of the fire, the blanket, the brisk scrubbing seeped through her chilled body. She opened her eyes, which were amber-brown and terrified.

She turned them from Kirke, who was rubbing her feet briskly to warm them, to Robin who stood behind her, scrubbing her hair dry.

"Oh," she whispered faintly, in a tone of such abject relief that Robin was startled. "I don't know who you are — but when I saw your lighted windows — "

She shuddered and was silent, and Kirke tucked her now warmed feet into bedroom slippers Robin had provided and smiled at her.

"You're all right now," he told her comfortingly. "I'm Kirke Bryant, and this is my sister, Robin."

The woman smiled faintly at both of

them. Now she could hold the coffee cup and drink the heartening liquid, and color began very slowly to come back to her lovely face.

"My car broke down," she said huskily. "Or rather, I ran out of gas. It was storming so, and I was terrified out there in that awful darkness alone, and I started walking." She shuddered and once more was silent as if the memory of that experience were too much to be borne.

"Well, don't worry about it now; you're quite all right," Kirke told her quickly. "Will the people who were expecting you — "

"Oh, nobody was expecting me," said the woman. "I'm Brooke Hildreth."

Obviously the name meant nothing to either of them, and she seemed to relax very slightly.

"I am on my way to visit my uncle Ezra Calloway, at Peacock Hill. Do you know the place?" she went on huskily.

"Well, of course I do. Why, I

sometimes work for Mr. Ezra," Kirke answered swiftly. "He's a fine old gentleman. He'll be worried."

The woman managed the faintest possible laugh.

"Can you really imagine Uncle Ezra being worried about anything that happened less than five hundred years ago, unless he's changed a lot since I last saw him, which was ten years ago? Has he changed?"

Kirke chuckled.

"He's still completely wrapped up in ancient history, Old World ancient history, if that's what you mean," he said. "But just the same, I imagine he'd be shaken out of that hobby of his if he knew you were on your way to visit him and were so late in arriving. It's only five miles or so from here to Peacock Hill."

The storm seemed to have renewed its assault, and Brooke shuddered and sank more deeply into her cocoon of blankets.

"He's not expecting me," she

answered. "I decided to surprise him. And I wouldn't go back into that storm for all the crown jewels of Old Russia!"

She looked from one to the other anxiously.

"Could I possibly stay here for the night?" she pleaded.

"Well, of course you're going to stay here as long as you want to and can put up with us," Robin said warmly.

"Of course you are," Kirke agreed. "And in the morning, I'll take some gas to your car and drive you to Peacock Hill."

Tears swam in Brooke's lovely eyes, though she tried to smile.

"You are both so heavenly kind!" she stammered. "I'd forgotten people could be so kind."

"Then you must have known some darned funny people, if they were the kind that wouldn't offer you shelter on a night like this," Robin told her firmly. "Now come along. I'll tuck you into bed, and you'll be fine in

9

the morning. Bet you won't even have a cold. These mountains are mighty healthy — fine climate, fresh air, the best of everything."

In the small, immaculate room to which Robin guided her, Brooke looked about her and asked hesitantly, "I'm not robbing you of your room, am I?"

Robin, turning down the thick, warm covers of the enormous bed that took up a considerable portion of the room, laughed.

"Oh, goodness, no," she answered gaily. "Kirke and I are very rich people. We have a spare room for guests, our own power plant for electricity and running water and an oil-burning furnace! People in the mountains sniff at us disdainfully and say things like 'A fool and his money'; but Kirke and I don't mind!"

Brooke managed a faint smile, and let Robin help her into the big bed.

"Thank you, Robin. Oh, thank you for everything!" she murmured, as the sleep of exhaustion swallowed her up.

"Oh, shucks!" said Robin cheerfully, and slipped quietly out of the room.

Brooke was asleep almost before the door closed behind Robin. As she came back into the main room of the house, she tripped over a sodden heap just inside the door. She picked it up, to discover that it was the fur coat that had slipped from Brooke's shoulders.

Robin picked up the coat, and her eyes widened. "Why, Kirke," she gasped, awed, "it's *mink*!"

"It would be," Kirke agreed dryly. "Probably just some old thing she puts on for second best, or even third or fourth. What else *would* a wealthy woman be wearing? And you want to bet the car she abandoned is a Cadillac or something even ritzier?"

Robin, spreading the coat gently to dry, stared at him.

"She's a wealthy widow?" she asked.

Kirke nodded, scowling. "I just remembered the name. She was married some time last fall. The bridegroom was kidnapped in some silly horseplay by his hilarious friends, and killed in a motor smashup trying to get back to start on their honeymoon. She was married and widowed in a matter of a couple of hours."

Her blue eyes enormous with shock and dismay, Robin gasped, "Oh, Kirke, how awful!"

"It was all of that," Kirke agreed grimly. "I remember reading about it in the newspapers. Because of the prominence of the bride and groom, the newspapers made a sort of field day out of it. I'd forgotten all about it until she mentioned her name. She hesitated — remember? She's probably had all the publicity about it she can stand, so now she's run off down here to visit Mr. Ezra. We mustn't let her find out that we know anything about it. She'll tell us what she wants us to know."

Robin nodded agreement.

2

THE storm had blown itself out by morning, though heavy, dark-looking clouds still clung to the mountain tops. But the rain had stopped and the air had a crisp bite to it, even though it was March and spring had already crept into the valleys below.

Robin and Kirke moved quietly as they had breakfast. Then Kirke climbed into the jeep to go hunt for the car Brooke had abandoned. The jeep carried a spare can of gas, and there was more in the pump house, so there would be no necessity of driving back to the filling station, halfway down the mountain.

He came upon the car, two miles or more from home. There was no mistaking it, of course. It was a long, low, sweeping Cadillac, two-toned green.

He was startled to discover that the keys were still in it; Brooke had not even locked it, although there was a full assortment of expensive luggage crowding the interior of the big car.

After filling the gas tank, he slid beneath the wheel and familiarized himself with its assortment of gadgets. The car started smoothly and he headed it toward the log house where its owner had taken refuge.

While he was retrieving the car, Robin slipped into the spare room where Brooke was just waking up. She yawned and stretched luxuriously — like Samanthy, Robin told herself, when she had had her good night bowl of milk and her babies were asleep.

"Oh, hello. I hope I didn't wake you," Robin said, as she saw that Brooke was awake.

"Heavens, I haven't slept like this in ages. What *is* this mattress stuffed with? I've never felt anything so soft."

"Goose feathers," Robin answered matter of factly, her pert little nose

14

wrinkling in amusement. "That's a featherbed, not a mattress."

Brooke lifted herself on her elbow and looked down at the bed.

"Well, so this is a featherbed," she mused. "I've often wondered what it was like to sleep on one — and now I know."

"Kirke got so used to hard beds in the army and then later in Saudi Arabia, that he will have nothing to do with featherbeds. Claims a hard mattress is better for one's back. Me, I was brought up sleeping in featherbeds in winter, and I still like 'em," Robin grinned. "Are you ready for breakfast? And what would you like?"

"Oh, whatever you and Kirke are having will be fine," Brooke answered.

Robin laughed. "Oh, Kirke and I had breakfast hours ago, and he's gone to find your car," she answered. "Your clothes aren't quite dry yet — that wool suit of yours takes a lot of drying. But I can lend you a robe, and when Kirke comes back, your luggage will be in

15

your car. But there's no point in your waiting that long for breakfast."

"Come to think of it, I'm starving," Brooke admitted frankly. "I can't remember having any dinner last night, though I think I had lunch."

"Oh, I'm sorry. I should have heated you some soup or a glass of milk or something before you went to bed," Robin apologized.

"I couldn't have eaten anything," Brooke assured her. "I was too exhausted and too frightened."

Robin, bringing a rose-colored chenille robe from her own room, nodded soberly.

"The mountains can be pretty scary at night when you aren't used to them, and the storm was pretty bad, too," she agreed. "I'll go start your breakfast, and you come along when you're ready."

Brooke sat on the side of the bed and looked down at the flannelette nightgown in which she was encased. She was several inches taller than Robin, and so the gown reached barely below her knees. The bedroom slippers were obviously Robin's best, because they were practically new, and matched in color the dull rose of the chenille robe.

Brooke found that the robe reached almost to her ankles, and as she knotted it about her slender waist she caught a glimpse of herself in the mirror of the big, old-fashioned bureau against one wall and laughed suddenly. And the sound of her laugh was so unaccustomed that she caught her breath, startled. She had actually laughed aloud, for the first time since David had died; the first time since that black night of horror had ungulfed her!

She drew a deep, hard breath, squared her shoulders and went out to the kitchen where Robin was waiting for her, gay and friendly. Brooke stared at the food on the table — a bowl of oatmeal, with a pitcher of thick yellow cream, a slice of home-cured ham waiting for the golden-yellow scrambled eggs Robin was beating in a big blue bowl.

"Oh, my goodness," Brooke gasped. "I never have more than just orange juice and coffee for breakfast."

Robin protested, "But this isn't really breakfast. This is that silly middle of the day meal people call brunch."

Brooke laughed and sat down. "Well, since I can't remember eating anything at all yesterday, and everything looks delicious — I'm starved."

"Well, hooray for you." Robin grinned at her. "As we say in the mountains, 'Set a spell and eat hearty'."

Brooke laughed and obeyed. Robin poured a cup of coffee for herself and sat down across the table, smiling as Brooke tasted the oatmeal, looked surprised and began eating with a healthy appetite.

"You must have been frightened to death last night," Robin said soberly. "I was born and brought up here, with five miserable years in the valley while Kirke was overseas. But I'd have been frightened to be lost in a storm like that one."

"I kept thinking I'd meet a bear or a panther or something," Brooke admitted. "Are there wild animals in these mountains?"

"Oh, I imagine so," Robin answered cautiously. "I never saw one, but you hear some pretty horrific stories sometimes; and there are occasionally loud animal cries at night not as far from the house as I'd like them to be."

"You have a dog, don't you?" asked Brooke.

Robin grinned impishly. "Samanthy doesn't care for dogs," she said cheerfully.

"Samanthy? Who's Samanthy?" asked Brooke curiously.

Robin indicated the big gray cat, surrounded by her family, that lay in a box in a corner of the kitchen. Brooke stared at the cat, who stared back at her coolly, as though not quite sure whether she was a friend or not.

"You let her dictate to you?" Brooke asked.

"Well, after all, it's her home, too," Robin pointed out reasonably. "She hated being away as much as I did. She was only a year old when she had to be 'farmed out' with a neighbour, while Kirke did his military service and then stayed three more years in Saudi Arabia in the oil fields. And when she came home last fall, she was so glad to be here that she stayed right under our feet for a month or two, afraid we'd go off and leave her again."

"Oh, now, Robin, you aren't going to tell me that she remembered you for five years?" Brooke protested.

"She did," Robin insisted firmly. "She's a very knowledgeable cat."

Brooke laughed, and once more the sound of her own laughter startled her.

"Cats do remember," Robin insisted stubbornly. "Haven't you read about them finding their way to their old owners who have moved off and left

20

them? Sometimes it takes them a year or two, but they do it. Samanthy could, I bet!"

"Then why didn't she follow you when you went to the valley to go to school!" asked Brooke teasingly.

"Because Kirke and I both left, and she couldn't make up her mind which of us she should follow," Robin answered. "And besides, I had a long talk with her the night before we left, and I promised her if she'd be a good cat and stay with the Brambletts and help their cat catch mice, Kirke and I would come home and bring her back here."

"You had a long talk with her?" teased Brooke.

"Well, of course. Cats are like people. I mean you can talk to them, reason with them, make them understand — if you love them enough," Robin insisted stubbornly.

Brooke smiled tremulously.

"You almost make me believe that, Robin," she admitted.

21

"Well, if you'd been around cats as much as I have, and loved them as much as I do, you'd know it was true," Robin said sturdily. "I've had cats and kittens even since I can remember. Once we had forty-two cats!"

"Good heavens!" gasped Brooke, thoroughly diverted from her own thoughts.

Robin nodded. "Dad used to say that we had forty acres of land, and that forty-two cats was only a little more than a cat to an acre. But we couldn't have any more, because that would crowd them." She chuckled, in fond memory. "He died when I was ten. I miss him very much."

"Of course you do, darling," said Brooke softly.

Robin became brisk. "What kind of jam or jelly or preserves would you like with that toast? And can I make you some more toast?"

"Gracious, no!" Brooke held up protesting hands, laughing. "I haven't eaten that much in ages! But it was delicious, and you're a wonderful cook, Robin."

Robin flushed with pleasure but made the usual disclaimer, "Oh, shucks! Anybody can scramble eggs and make toast. Wait until you've eaten one of my dinners before you decide whether I can cook or not. I do hope you will come and have dinner with us sometime."

"Just ask me, Robin — any time at all. I hate to think about leaving. I wish I dared ask you to take me in as a boarder for the next fifty years — only I'd probably be a nuisance," Brooke answered.

"We'd love having you, not as a boarder but as a house guest, on a permanent basis," Robin told her. "And if you and Mr. Ezra 'have words', you come and stay with us."

Brooke stared at her.

"You think that's likely — I mean that we'll 'have words'?" she asked uneasily. "I haven't seen him in ten years; and I never knew him well at all. And I've never been here before.

Maybe he won't want to be bothered with me."

"I can't imagine anybody not wanting to 'be bothered' with you and I can't think of your being a bother," Robin protested with such warm sincerity that Brooke was touched and pleased. "But if you aren't happy there, you come right straight back here and we'll *love* having you! And that's for sure."

"Thanks, darling — you're a lamb," said Brooke, misty-eyed and her smile tremulous. "Here, let me help with the dishes. Better still, let me wash them."

"Oh, we just chuck 'em in the automatic dishwater," said Robin rather grandly, "and forget about 'em. I bet I'm the only woman on Big Hungry Mountain who has an automatic dishwater *and* a washing machine!"

"My word, you *are* a lucky girl." Brooke was suitably impressed. "Big Hungry? Is that the name of this mountain? What an ugly name?"

Robin nodded soberly. "A settlement

of whites was starved out by Indians a hundred or more years ago. And the name the Indians had for the mountain was one the white people couldn't pronounce, so they just called it Big Hungry, because of the settlement that was starved out."

Brooke nodded understandingly and watched Robin's piquant face, with its tip-tilted nose, that wrinkled gaily when she laughed.

"You love the mountains, don't you, Robin?" Her tone made it a statement, not a question.

"I can't imagine anybody in his right mind who wouldn't," Robin answered swiftly, and added cautiously, "If I tell you something, will you promise to keep it a secret?"

Brooke said, "Cross my heart, Robin."

"The most miserably unhappy five years of my life were those I spent down in the valley with Aunt Grace, while Kirke was overseas," said Robin frankly. "I don't want him to know it, because he thought I was blissfully happy. He had to go into the army, of course, and then when he had finished his service, there was this chance for him to go to Saudi Arabia and work in the oil fields at perfectly fantastic, utterly incredible wages. He knew that if he stayed there three years, we'd have enough money saved up to take care of us comfortably, with the odd jobs he'd be sure to pick up around these parts. He's a master mechanic of all sorts of machinery, and then, too, we'd 'live at home' — raise all our food, just about. But if he had known I wasn't perfectly satisfied with Aunt Grace, he'd have come kiting home pronto! So I wrote him about what a marvellous time I was having, the dates and the pretty clothes, so he stayed. That's why I don't want him to know I had a perfectly miserable time."

Brooke asked gently, "Your Aunt wasn't kind to you?"

Robin looked startled. "Aunt Grace? Oh, she was grand to me. She loved having me, and we had fun. It was just

26

that I missed the mountains so much it was like an ache inside of me! But now I'm home again, and Kirke's here, and Samanthy's here and her family, and life's pretty grand."

"I'm so glad, Robin," said Brooke. "But what if Kirke should decide to get married?"

"Oh, there'd still be room for me here," Robin boasted happily. "Kirke wouldn't marry a girl who wouldn't be good friends with me. It's pretty lonely up here in the wintertime, and she'd probably be glad to have me. But if she wasn't — well, I'd pitch a tent down there by the spring and take Samanthy and her family with me, and we'd he happy as crickets."

"I'll bet you would, too." Brooke laughed again. "But suppose *you* fall in love and want to get married?"

"He'd have to be a mountain man, and then he and Kirke would be friends," Robin said cheerfully, completely undisturbed.

3

WHEN Robin looked out of the window a little later and saw Kirke easing the big car carefully down the narrow, winding road, her eyes widened.

"Is that your car?" she gasped.

"Yes," Brooke answered, and was puzzled by her awe. "Why? Don't you like Cadillacs?"

"May the saints preserve us!" Robin murmured. "How would the likes of me know whether I like 'em or not? I've seen one or two, but neither the mountains here nor the valley go in for 'em. Jeeps are much more our style."

Kirke got out of the car, closed the door carefully, stood for a moment eyeing the gleaming thing and then turned and came into the house where Robin and Brooke were waiting for him.

There was a twinkle in his eyes as he bowed very low to Brooke and dropped the car keys into her hand.

"Ma'am," he spoke deliberately in the mountain twang and idiom, "us folks here on Big Hungry all thank you right kindly."

Brooke stared at him, wide-eyed.

"For what?" she asked, deeply puzzled.

"For the confidence you have displayed in our honesty," he answered, and turned to Robin. "Would you believe me if I told you she left the car keys in the car, the doors unlocked and a stack of very expensive-looking luggage in her car?"

"Well, why not?" Robin seemed almost as puzzled as Brooke. "Nobody up here would touch anything in the car — or bother the car itself."

Kirke grinned warmly.

"You know that, Small Fry, and I know it — but how did a gal from the wicked city know it? I claim she had a very flattering faith in us."

Brooke interrupted, "Frankly, I never

29

gave it a thought. I was terrified, all alone there in the dark, in that terrible storm, with no gas. I wasn't interested in a single thing except getting somewhere where there was people! And all along the road I expected some sort of evil beast to pounce out at me. I ran most of the way, I think — miles and miles; and then I saw your lights — " She broke off, shuddering as the memory of the blackness and terror spread through her again.

"Miles and miles?" Kirke twitted her gently, a twinkle in his eyes. "It's exactly a mile and five-eighths to where I left the jeep. And now I'll go back and get it."

"You aren't going to walk?" Brooke protested.

Kirke seemed surprised at the question.

"Well, of course. I have to drive the jeep back."

"Then wait until I get some clothes on and I'll drive you back there,"

30

Brooke insisted eagerly. "Could I have the wardrobe case out of my car?"

"Of course. But it's no walk at all back to the jeep."

"Please! I want to drive you back," Brooke told him.

"Sure — thanks," said Kirke, smiling at her eagerness, as he went out to the car. "Which is the wardrobe case? I'm just an ignorant back-woodsman, remember."

Brooke called from the doorway, shivering in the damp raw wind, "The biggest one."

"It would be," Kirke murmured to himself as he hauled out the case and brought it into the house and put it down in the room where Brooke had slept.

"I won't be a minute." Brooke thanked him warmly and closed the door.

Kirke went on into the kitchen, where Robin was waiting for him with a pot of steaming coffee.

"Isn't she beautiful, Kirke? Did you

31

ever see anybody so beautiful?" Robin asked, while Kirke spooned thick yellow cream into his coffee and stirred it thoughtfully.

"Oh, yes, she's lovely," he agreed.

"And she's so — well, so sweet and friendly — and not a bit high-hat or snooty like you'd expect a woman who wears a mink coat and drives a Cadillac to be," Robin rushed on. "We've had such a good time getting acquainted. Do you think maybe we could ask her over for dinner, if she stays awhile at Peacock Hill?"

Kirke looked up at her sharply.

"Small Fry, are you lonely here?" he demanded so unexpectedly that for a moment she could not answer him. "Sure you don't want to go back down to the valley?"

"Don't you dare say that, unless you want your mouth washed out with soap and water," she flashed at him hotly. "Lonely? With you here? And Samanthy and her family? And the cow and the chickens and the pigs?"

Kirke was studying her with a sharp intensity.

"You don't miss all the fun, the pretty clothes, the dates, the good times you wrote me about?"

Robin colored hotly and turned away.

"I don't miss any of them a bit," she informed him, and there was such sincerity in her voice that he was comforted.

"There's something that bothers me a little," he said at last.

Robin turned swiftly, apprehension in her eyes.

"About me?"

Kirke nodded. "After all, you're going on nineteen, and we can't have an old maid in the family," he drawled. "'Twouldn't be nowise fittin' for a Bryant gal to go unwed to her nineteenth birthday."

Robin laughed. "Well, never you mind about that, pal!" she mocked. "Time comes for me to wed, I'll round me up a feller, you wait and see. And he'll be a mountain man, or I'll have no truck with him a-tall, a-tall!"

Brooke came back, slim and smart and lovely in a jade green wool dress, slim brown alligator pumps on her feet, her hair combed into exquisite order.

"You two seem very merry. Is it a private joke?"

"My esteemed brother is getting very worried because he's about to have an old maid sister on his hands." Robin chuckled. "He wants me to go down to the valley and hunt me up a husband. As if I'd waste a second glance on a man who was content to live at the foot of a mountain instead of on top of one!"

"Oh, well, there are a few unmarried mountain men about," Kirke grinned as he stood up. "One of these days I'll take my squirrel gun out and round one up for you."

Robin's eyes rounded in mock admiration.

"If there's anything in this world I've always hankered for, it's to be the bride in a shotgun wedding," she pointed out.

"I wouldn't worry about her getting married, Kirke," said Brooke, and all laughter, all happiness was gone from her lovely face. "Maybe she'd be much better off if she never got involved in anything so silly as being in love."

Startled, she caught their glances and colored hotly as she turned toward the door.

"Shall we go? I should arrive at Peacock Hill some time today. How much farther is it?" She tossed the words over her shoulder as Kirke followed her out to the car, while Robin stood on the wide old verandah, watching.

"It's no more than a whoop and a holler," Kirke told her. When Brooke looked at him, frowning, he grinned. "Around three more curves in the road. Two miles as the crow flies — about five as your Cadillac travels."

Brooke nodded and slid beneath the wheel as Kirke got in beside her. He had turned the car around so that she had only to drive carefully up the winding, narrow lane to the road. They reached the road, turned east, and came to a wide sweeping parking place that jutted out over the mountain below.

"You'll have to turn here," Kirke told her. "There isn't another 'turn-out' until you get halfway down the mountain."

Brooke nodded as she guided the car into the semicircle that would bring it back to the road and headed west. When she had reached the middle of the semicircle, she stopped the car and sat for a moment, looking wide-eyed at the magnificent sweep of scenery spread out below.

"Takes your breath away, doesn't it?" said Kirke. He got out of the car and held out his hand to her, taking it for granted she would want to feast her eyes on every detail of that scene before she left it.

The mountain dropped sheer here,

beneath the great ledge that had been made a spot for parking, so people would stop and admire the wonderful view. Below them, dropping straight down, there were giant trees, great firs with their eternal green, hardwoods leafless in the raw, damp March wind. At the foot of the mountain, a stream fought its way across and around and between huge black rocks that turned its rushing waters into foam-laced spray. On the other side of the river, another mountain rose as sheer as the one on which they stood, with great outcroppings of black rock, and with more firs and hardwoods climbing the steep side. At the very top, perched like an eagle's nest, there was a house that at that distance looked like a child's white toy, tossed down after play. Down where the Valley stream ran across this road, stood a big gaunt-looking old house that once had been painted yellow and that even now held a faint glow of color despite the gray day.

"The old grist mill," Kirke answered

Brooke's question. "And the patches above are Sam Enslee's garden patches. He has an apple orchard up there, and in spring when the trees are in bloom it looks as if someone had spread out a pale pink quilt to dry."

"And the white house up at the top of that mountain?"

"Oh, those are summer people from the lowlands," Kirke answered, and it seemed to Brooke that there was the faintest possible edge to his tone, as though he had little admiration for summer people. "They wanted a view — so they built their house there! They got a view, but they also have a terrific repair bill every summer when they want to come up for a few months."

"It must be worth it," Brooke said slowly, and looked again at the grist mill, glimmering faintly in the murky light. "But mountains make me feel so unimportant. I don't think I'd like living in an eagle's nest like that white one."

She turned her head and looked up at him.

"You must have missed all this terribly while you were in Saudi Arabia," she probed gently.

Kirke smiled. "Oh, yes, of course, but I had decided that as soon as I'd put aside enough money I would come back here and never leave again. If you've got something like that to look forward to, something to hope for — well, you get through the waiting."

Brooke nodded, still eyeing him curiously. "But what do you do for amusement? I should think you'd be terribly bored, just working all the time."

Kirke's eyes cooled ever so slightly, but his smile was still warm and friendly.

"Neither Robin nor I work all the time," he pointed out. "There are, of course, things we have to do. But we often drive down to the city on Saturday afternoons to shop, have dinner at the restaurant down there, go to the movies. We have an excellent T.V., which Robin calls our window on the outside world. We go to church on Sundays, and there are barn dances, barn raisings. Oh, we live a very giddy social life, I assure you."

Brooke looked up at him, flushing.

"I didn't mean to be offensive," she apologized.

"You were not, at all," Kirke assured her pleasantly. "If you are planning to stay long at Peacock Hill, it's only natural that you would be interested in whatever facilities there are for entertaining yourself. Had you planned to stay long?"

"I don't quite know," Brooke admitted hesitantly. "I'm not sure Uncle Ezra will want me or even have room for me."

Kirke laughed aloud at that.

"There'll be no question about room," he told her. "Peacock Hill has eighteen bedrooms and five baths, besides your uncle's library and private sitting room and the main ballroom and all the other space."

Brooke stared at him, wide-eyed.

"But for goodness sake, why would Uncle Ezra, who has no family because he never married, want a huge place like that?" she marveled.

"Now that is something I suppose we'll never know," Kirke said.

Brooke seemed scarcely to hear him. Her eyes were on the vistas spread before them, and after a moment she spoke again.

"He used to spend the summers in Maine. And in the winters he would come to New York, move into a hotel in midtown where the museums and the library were easily accessible, and work. Mother and I went to dinner with him once or twice. That was ten years ago, and he never seemed to remember who we were. He's really my great-uncle, you know; Mother's uncle. He's terribly old, isn't he?"

"Oh, in years I suppose he must be in his eighties," Kirke agreed. "But mentally he's quite young. I suppose his hobby keeps him that way; keeps his mind alert, anyway."

He followed the direction of her eyes beneath the glowering March sky and said impulsively, "It's really quite beautiful when spring breaks. The woods are a new green, and along those black rocks across the river, you can see the wild azaleas breaking into bloom, and later the rhododendrons, and the mountain laurel, which the folks here call 'calico flower'. The yarb doctors get busy gathering ginseng root and all the medicinal herbs that grow in the mountains."

Brooke looked up at him, puzzled.

"You really love it up here, don't you?" she asked.

"Very much," he told her briefly, and turned back to the car. "Well, shall we get going? It may start raining again any minute."

4

THE jeep started off up the road, traveling slowly because of the narrowness of the winding road, and Brooke drove behind it. A mile or two beyond the Bryant homestead, tall wrought iron gates stood open before a winding drive. And as the jeep turned between the gates Brooke saw that, beautifully worked in the gates, were giant peacocks and the words "Peacock Hill."

The drive wound upward, to an enormous gray stone house that fitted into the landscape, its back against the mountain, as though it had grown there. Although Kirke had warned her it was a large place, she was not quite prepared for its stately if somewhat shabby appearance.

Kirke parked the jeep at the edge of the drive and came back to Brooke.

"I'll go in and find Mrs. Thrailkill, your uncle's housekeeper," he told her. "This time of the day she's in the back of the house somewhere, and there is no doorbell or knocker. Everybody uses the back entrance. But Mrs. Thrailkill would be upset if a relative of Mr. Ezra's made her first entrance into the house at the back!"

Brooke tried to smile, and nodded as he walked around the wide sweep of drive and disappeared at the back. She looked about her at this spot her eccentric uncle had chosen for his home.

The tall trees were bare, save for a group of towering cedars and some pines that grew down the slope at the back of the house. She had never experienced such silence; to a girl born and bred in the city, there was something almost ominous in the hush.

Meanwhile Kirke had crossed the back porch and knocked at the kitchen door. A moment later it swung open and a tall, lanky, weather-worn man stood there in battered overalls and an old sweater.

"Well, now, Kirke Bryant, you don't have to knock boy," he greeted Kirke warmly, and stood back, swinging the door open. "Come right in. Maw, here's Kirke. What's wrong? What kind of machinery's acting up now?"

Mrs. Thrailkill, nearly as tall as her husband, Elijah, her dark cotton dress immaculate beneath a gingham apron, rose from the table where she and her husband had been having their mid-day meal.

"Why, Kirke, I'm glad to see you, but who sent for you?" she asked. "You're just in time for dinner. Come in."

Kirke laughed. "Can't I ever come calling without being sent for?" he protested. "No, I've brought you some company. Mr. Ezra's niece is outside in her car."

Elijah and his wife exchanged swift, startled glances.

45

"Mr. Ezra's niece? Why, what in tarnation would a woman like that want here?" protested Elijah.

"Mr. Ezra's grand-niece, if you want to be technical about it," Kirke amended. "She ran out of gas on the road last night and put up with Robin and me until this morning, when I could get some gas in the car. She's come to spend a few days, I believe, although she has baggage enough to spend the whole summer. You'll like her, Bessie; she's a very nice person. May I bring her in?"

Considerably flustered, Mrs. Thrailkill said hurriedly, "Well, yes, of course. Is the front door key in the lock, Lije?"

"Well, now, where else would it be except where it belongs?" her husband wanted to know, affronted.

"I could bring her around here," Kirke suggested.

"Don't you dare!" Mrs. Thrailkill protested sharply. "Come along, Kirke. We mustn't keep her sitting out there in the cold."

46

She led the way out of the kitchen, through the swinging door into the vast reception hall and to the front door, calling over her shoulder, "Lije, you come and help with the baggage, and turn up that thermostat. Its colder than Alaska in here."

She struggled with the enormous key in the ancient lock of the big oak-paneled front door and finally managed to get it open. She shivered as the raw March wind struck her flushed face, and hurried down to the Cadillac where Brooke stood waiting, obviously uncertain of her welcome.

"Brooke, this is Mrs. Thrailkill, your uncle's housekeeper," Kirke introduced them. "Miss Bessie, this is Mrs. Hildreth."

"I'm right proud to meet you, ma'am," said Miss Bessie, and offered her hand. "And I'm awful glad you've come to visit. It'll do Mr. Ezra a sight of good to see some of his kinfolks."

"That's very kind of you, Mrs. Thrailkill." Brooke was touched and warmed by the welcome. "I do hope I'm not going to be a bother or upset things."

"Upset things? Why, sakes alive, ma'am, we're that glad to see you," Miss Bessie insisted eagerly. As Elijah came out, she waved at him and said, "This is my husband Elijah, Mrs. Hildreth. He and Kirke will look after your luggage. Come right in out of this cold wind."

"Of course," she went on busily as they crossed the drive and went up the steps and into the house, "it's not a sight warmer here in the front of the house than it is outdoors. But we just use a part of the house: Mr. Ezra's study and his suite, and the kitchen quarters. Lije and I see to it that part of the house is warm."

Brooke looked about her at the huge reception hall with its black and white tiled floor, the graceful swoop of an enormous staircase, a huge living room glimpsed through an open door, and blinked.

"I had no idea the place was so huge," she said.

"It is that, ma'am," Miss Bessie agreed, "for just a lone old man like Mr. Ezra. But he likes his privacy, and seems as if he couldn't feel private-like in a smaller place."

"Where is he?" asked Brooke curiously.

"In his own quarters," Miss Bessie answered. "Lije took him and Mr. Alden their lunch a while ago, and he said they were working up a storm and didn't want to be interrupted again until they rang."

She hesitated, frowning, and then added, "Well, maybe it would be all right to let him know you are here."

"No, don't bother them," Brooke cut in hastily. "I doubt if he will remember me. I haven't seen him in ten years; and he may not want me around. Let's wait until he rings, shall we?"

"Well, maybe that would be better," Miss Bessie said with frank relief, and turned as Elijah and Kirke came in laden with the baggage. "Take 'em upstairs, Lije. I think maybe the room on the left at the top of the stairs. It's got its own bathroom and a dressing room and sitting room and a wonderful view over the mountains."

As the men started up the stairs, Miss Bessie drew Brooke down the hall and into the kitchen.

"Sit here and thaw out," she urged hospitably, and cleared a place at the table.

"Oh, I've disturbed your lunch," Brooke protested.

"Shucks, Lije and me are delighted you did," said Miss Bessie, and it was obvious she meant it. "Soon as Kirke comes down, we'll make him come and eat, too. It's not much, but such as it is, there's plenty of it. Here, have some hot coffee. That'll warm you up quicker than anything."

Brooke felt as though she were being wrapped in a warm cloak that shut out all the panic and loneliness and uneasiness that had beset her for so long.

Kirke and Elijah came in together, laughing, and Kirke smiled at her as Miss Bessie hospitably urged him to a seat at the table.

"Thanks, Miss Bessie, but Robin would just about murder me if I didn't come home for dinner," Kirke protested, and told Brooke, "You'll be all right now."

Brooke's smile was tremulous as she nodded. "Oh, yes, I'll be all right now," she agreed.

"Well, I should hope so," Miss Bessie said vigorously. "My, it's going to be nice to have somebody young and pretty in the house."

"Take good care of her, Miss Bessie," said Kirke. And to Brooke, "Robin and I will look forward to having you drop in any time you're so inclined, Mrs. Hildreth."

Brooke winced. "Oh, don't call me Mrs. Hildreth," she protested so sharply that all three looked at her, startled. She flushed and added quickly, "You make me feel like a stranger. My name is Brooke!"

Robin was waiting anxiously for him when he came into the house.

"Golly, you were gone so long I was about to call out a posse with bloodhounds to hunt for you," she greeted him.

"I showed Brooke the way to Peacock Hill and helped Lije unload her luggage," Kirke answered, as he went to the kitchen sink to wash his hands, while Robin dished up their mid-day meal.

She paused, staring at him.

"You call her Brooke?" she marveled.

"She asked me to," Kirke answered. "She doesn't like to be called Mrs. Hildreth."

Robin nodded soberly as she finished her task.

"I guess it does sort of remind her of him," she admitted. "Did Mr. Ezra welcome her with open arms? If he didn't, I'll want to cook him up a nice mess of toadstools and call 'em mushrooms."

"Mr. Ezra was not available," Kirke chuckled. "Seems he and Alden are all tied up and didn't want to be disturbed. But Miss Bessie and Lije were tickled pink to have some company. They'll see to it she has a wonderful time. At least they'll see to her physical comfort, and that's about all anybody can do for her now."

"She's a darling, isn't she?" said Robin happily. "I hope she'll come to see us now and then while she's here."

"I have a strong hunch that she'll be here only a few days, no more," Kirke answered. "Somehow I can't quite picture her settling down for any lengthy stay at Peacock Hill, can you?"

"Well, no, I guess you have to be mountain-bred to like it here this time of year," Robin agreed reluctantly. "What a shame she didn't wait until May or June to come, when the azaleas and the rhododendrons and the apple orchards are in bloom."

"And the snakes are stirring," Kirke mocked lightly.

"Kirke," she began awkwardly and he saw that she was deadly serious, "can I ask you something?"

"*May*, not *can*," Kirke corrected her, puzzled by her solemnity. "You *may* ask me whatever you like; but I don't guarantee I'll answer you."

"I'm serious, Kirke," she insisted. "Please don't joke."

"Sorry, Small Fry." He became as serious as she. "Ask me anything you like, honey, and if I can, I'll answer it."

"Kirke, would you like to get married?" she asked.

Kirke almost choked on the forkful of green beans he had just put into his mouth and stared at her, completely astounded.

"My sainted aunt in Paradise!" he gasped. "Whatever put that cockeyed thought into your crazy little head?"

"Brooke," she answered simply. "I guess maybe I was just so happy to be here with you that it didn't occur to me I might be standing in your way, keeping you from getting married, having your own family. Am I, Kirke?"

Kirke was staring at her incredulously.

"Well, of all the crazy — Small Fry, whom would I marry, in the very unlikely event that I'd want to? I don't know any marriageable females," he protested.

"Oh, sure you do," Robin insisted. "There's Stella Ames, down at the schoolhouse; and Elvira Rogers, the artist gal who comes up here every summer to paint, and who makes eyes at you until I wonder she doesn't go blind; and Mary Blake, the minister's daughter who teaches Sunday School. Oh, there are scads of girls who'd just about jump out of their skins at the very thought of marrying you."

Kirke saw that she was quite in earnest, and suddenly he laughed as he buttered a corn muffin.

55

"You know something, Robin?" he asked after a moment.

"Not very much, I'm afraid," she admitted huskily.

"You are really the most unpredictable little female it's ever been my good fortune to meet," he told her firmly. "I never know when you're going to break out in another direction. But this idea of marrying me off — look, Small Fry, cease and desist! If I want to get married, I can handle the matter without your help."

Robin flushed. "Well, it was only that I wanted you to know that any time you do get married, it will be all right with me," she told him.

Kirke raised his eyebrows slightly.

"Well, that's real big of you!" he mocked.

"I mean I can move out of the house if you want to bring a wife here," she went on earnestly.

"Can you now? Where to, or mustn't I ask that question?"

"Oh, I could pitch a tent down by

the creek and take Samanthy and her family with me."

"That ought to be very comfortable, until you froze to death."

"Or I could fix a place in the barn with Muley."

Kirke's twinkle died and he leaned toward her earnestly.

"Look, Small Fry, in the not at all likely event that I should decide to take unto myself a wife, you'd move nowhere!" he told her quietly. "This place belongs to us jointly. It's as much yours as mine. And any woman I'd want to marry would love you as much as I do — or I darned well wouldn't marry her! Is that clear?"

She nodded soberly. "And if I want to get married — and believe me, I'm not even *about* to think of it — it would be the same."

"It would have to be, of course."

She was silent for a long moment, while Kirke studied her.

"It was Brooke who brought all this up?" he suggested at last.

"Yes. Kirke, isn't she beautiful? Like a movie star — only even more beautiful." Robin glowed and added, "And she's not a bit snippy or haughty the way I thought all society women were."

Kirke laughed. "Honey, you've been going to the wrong movies," he pointed out. "Rich women, even beautiful rich women like Brooke, are just people."

"Are they really, Kirke?" asked Robin wonderingly.

5

MISS BESSIE straightened and looked about the big bedroom, now warm and cozy from the small heater in a corner. Each of the huge bedrooms had gas heaters, so that they need not be warmed unless they were in use, and this one had been burning since Brooke's arrival.

Everything was in order, and Miss Bessie smiled at Brooke.

"There now," she said happily. "I guess everything is straight. I do hope you'll be comfortable, Mrs. Hildreth."

"Please call me Brooke," she begged. "And I'm sure I'll be quite comfortable. I'm so sorry to have put you to so much trouble, Mrs. Thrailkill."

"Most folks call me Miss Bessie, Miss Brooke," said Miss Bessie comfortably. "And it wasn't a bit of trouble! I enjoyed it. Lije and I get bone-lazy just waiting on two old men. I don't mean to sound disrespectful. Mr. Ezra is a grand gentleman and kind as can be; and Mr. Alden, his secretary, is only a few years younger. My, they do enjoy arguing with each other. Such good friends they are."

She glanced at the sea of luggage and asked, "Would you like me to help you unpack?"

"Oh, no thanks, you've done quite enough." Brooke smiled at her. "It will give me something to do until dinner time."

Miss Bessie hesitated and said awkwardly, "There is something that will probably seem pretty silly to you, Miss Brooke, but I'll warn you. Mr. Ezra always insists on dressing for dinner, and if you have a formal gown that needs pressing — "

Brooke stared at her.

"Dressing for dinner? Miss Bessie, you don't mean white tie and tails, surely?" she gasped.

"That's just what I mean, Miss

60

Brooke," she admitted. "He has his breakfast and his lunch on a tray in his suite with Mr. Alden. But for dinner, he insists on dressing; there must be candles on the table, and flowers, and Lije in a white coat, serving, even when it's only Mr. Ezra and Mr. Alden. And it's nearly always only Mr. Ezra and Mr. Alden. Peacock Hill doesn't have many guests. I've been here ten years, ever since Mr. Ezra bought the Hill, and I could count on the fingers of one hand the times we've had folks in to dinner. So if you'd like me to press something — "

Brooke shook her head.

"Thanks, but I'm sure I can find something in my luggage," she answered. "I have to admit I'm not sure I packed my formal evening wear, because I didn't think I'd need it here. But if I do — "

"You will, Miss Brooke, every evening as long as you are here," Miss Bessie assured her, and turned to the door. "Well, I'll get along and start dinner.

Mr. Ezra's right fussy about dinner. If you need me, there's a bell-push there that rings in the kitchen, and I'll come right along."

"Thanks, Miss Bessie, but I'm sure I'll be quite all right," Brooke thanked her.

"Dinner's at seven, Miss Brooke, and Mr. Ezra is very impatient if it's a minute late," Miss Bessie warned her.

"I'll be sitting in the drawing room with my hands folded in my lap and a bright smile pinned to my face five minutes before seven, I promise," Brooke answered. Miss Bessie gave her rich, warm laugh and went out, closing the door neatly behind her.

There was a vast cedar-lined closet in the dressing room, and she hung her belongings away, leaving out a dress to wear to dinner: a sheer gossamery thing of silver-gray with a short ballerina skirt and a snugly fitted bodice. It would have to do, she told herself as she tossed it on the bed, found the slippers of violet satin that complemented it, and that matched the wide stole of violet chiffon.

When she had completed her unpacking, she showered and dressed. At exactly five minutes of seven she came down the wide, curving staircase and heard voices in the big drawing room. She glanced again at her watch, saw that she was not late, and went on into the room.

Two men stood with cocktail glasses in hand, and she had a moment to examine them. One was tall, spare, with thick white hair and black-rimmed spectacles that gave his lean, pale face an almost owlish look. The other was younger, not quite so tall, a little heavier, and it was he who saw her first. His eyes widened and he broke off in mid-speech, as the older man, puzzled, turned to follow the direction of his eyes.

The two men stared at Brooke in her frail misty gray draperies, her copper-colored hair like a flame above the mist. Brooke smiled.

"Good evening, Uncle Ezra," she said quietly.

The taller man looked startled, but he gave her a small, old-fashioned bow and answered politely, "Why, good evening, my dear. Do I know you?"

"I'm your niece, Brooke, Uncle Ezra," she answered.

He scowled in bewilderment.

"My dear, you couldn't possibly be my niece," he protested. "You're a mere child. My niece would be at least forty-five."

Brooke laughed. "How she would hate you for saying that! She's a permanent thirty-two," she answered. "I'm really your great-niece, Uncle Ezra — Mark's and Eleanor's daughter. I met you when you were in New York the last time, but that was ten years ago. You've probably forgotten all about me, so it was very presumptuous of me to stop off to see you."

"Presumptuous? What an absurd thought!" the old man protested. "Why, I'm delighted, my child. Mark

64

and Eleanor's daughter Brooke. Well, well, my dear, this *is* a surprise and a very great pleasure."

"You don't mind my coming?" she asked.

"Mind? Why, what a ridiculous thought! I'm charmed, enchanted. It's delightful of you to remember me," said Ezra, and held her hand in his as he turned her toward the other man. "Tom, this is my very lovely great-niece. Tom is my oldest and best friend, Brooke, my dear. I couldn't manage without him. Mr. Alden, Miss Calloway."

He frowned as he spoke the name and looked swiftly at Brooke.

"Don't I remember that you were married a few months ago? I seem to remember shopping for a wedding present, didn't I?" he asked.

"You did, Uncle Ezra dear, and it was very beautiful!" Brooke answered, and managed huskily, "my husband was killed in a car accident a few hours after our wedding. If you don't mind, I'd rather not talk about it."

"My dear child," Ezra's voice was warm and tender, his arm about her shoulders very gentle, "of course not. We won't mention it again. I'm so terribly sorry."

Lije, in an immaculate white coat, appeared in the doorway just as the stately old grandfather clock in the hall gave out seven mellow deep-toned 'bongs.'

"Dinner is served," announced Lije, and Brooke told herself that no English butler with many years service to 'the quality' could have been more formally correct.

Ezra offered his arm to Brooke, and feeling as though she walked through some incredible movie scene, Brooke allowed herself to be guided out of the big drawing room, down the hall and into a dining room that could have comfortably seated forty guests. The table, in the center of the room, was like a small white oasis, shining with crystal goblets, the finest of old silver, heirloom china, and in the center a low bowl of pink and white blooms that gave off a faint but exquisite fragrance.

Ezra seated Brooke ceremoniously, and as he returned to his own place, she leaned forward to sniff that delicate fragrance.

"But where in the world did they come from? And what are they?" she cried. "I've never seen anything so lovely."

"Freesias, aren't they, Elijah?" asked Ezra, smiling at Brooke's delight.

"Yes, Mr. Ezra," Lije answered. "They've done right well this year."

"Right well?" Brooke's tone dismissed the words as totally inadequate. "They're gorgeous. But surely you didn't raise them here?"

"Oh, yes, in the conservatory." Ezra smiled proudly. "You must show Miss Brooke around the conservatory, Elijah."

"I'll be glad to, Mr. Ezra." Lije smiled and glided out of the room, the first course served.

Brooke dipped her spoon into the soup, tasted and looked wide-eyed at a smiling, urbane Ezra who was obviously enjoying her surprise.

"Uncle Ezra," she demanded, "is this turtle soup?"

"Of course," he replied.

"But where in the world — I mean — I don't mean to be rude — but clear turtle soup *here*!"

Ezra laughed.

"Oh, Tom and I are very fond of good food, as we see no reason we shouldn't have it, as long as it can be flown here, packed in dry ice, once a month," he told her. "Tom goes up to Asheville and picks up the carton, and we have a huge freezer that takes care of it until we are ready to use it."

There was a twinkle in his eyes, and he leaned toward her and lowered his voice to a conspiratorial whisper. "The difficult thing was teaching Miss Bessie what to do with it after she got her hands on it. She and Elijah feel that turnip greens and what is known colloquially as 'sow belly' should form the basis of all edible food. I think she had some doubts as to our sanity, but Tom and I have fond hopes of one day persuading her that snails, properly prepared, make delicious eating."

Dinner was delicious, carefully prepared and served with distinction by Elijah. Later, when they were having coffee in the big drawing room, with Brooke installed behind the lovely old coffee service, Ezra lit a cigar and smiled at her.

"And now, my dear, tell me about yourself," he suggested pleasantly. "Mark and Eleanor — how are they?"

"I really don't know." Brooke's lovely mouth was a thin line. "Father is living in South America with his fourth wife; Rio I think, though I'm not sure. And Mother is in the south of France, or was at the time of my wedding, with her third husband. Neither of them could come to the wedding, by the way, but they sent handsome checks."

Tom and Ezra were staring at her, and she looked up at them, a faint, twisted smile on her lips, her eyes bleak.

"I'm sorry, Uncle Ezra — "

"Sorry? My dear child, I am at a loss for words! But I'm very pleased, my dear, that you came here to me. And I sincerely hope you will stay as long as you can stand it. Tom and I are a couple of old fogies, and I'm afraid we wouldn't know the first thing about entertaining a lovely child like you; but there must be young people around the mountains. Aren't there, Tom?"

"I've met two that are completely delightful," Brooke answered before Tom could. "I was lost in the storm last night when my car ran out of gas, and I took refuge with Kirke and Robin Bryant. They were very kind."

"Kirke Bryant? Oh, yes, he's a very fine young man," said Ezra eagerly. "I don't think I've met his wife, have I, Tom?"

"Robin isn't his wife; she's his

70

sister," Brooke once more answered before Tom could. "I'd like you to know her, Uncle Ezra. She's really a darling."

"Oh, I'm afraid I'm not much for social activities, my dear," Ezra protested hurriedly, and she could see a momentary panic in his eyes. "I want you to feel perfectly at home here, and invite anyone you like at any time — but don't expect Tom or me to be visible until dinner time. We are very busy all day."

"Darling," Brooke protested, "I know all about your cherished privacy, and I wouldn't for worlds invade it any more than I've already done, by coming here myself. I wouldn't have come if I had dreamed that I would disturb you."

"Nonsense, my dear," protested Ezra. "We're delighted you did come. This is your home, my dear, as long as you want it to be."

"You're sweet, Uncle Ezra." And there was a mist of tears in her eyes as she smiled at him. "I've never had a real home."

"No, I suppose not," Ezra agreed.

"I think," said Brooke, rising, "if you don't want any more coffee, I'll say goodnight. I'm rather tired."

6

BROOKE awoke in the morning to a thin, watery sunlight spilling through the windows, and realized she hadn't slept so soundly since that ugly scene with David, that had once and for all destroyed the frail fabric of the love she had felt for him. She didn't even want to think about David, she reminded herself, taut-lipped, as she slipped out of bed and across to close the window. And then she drew a deep breath and turned away, yawning and stretching with an odd new sense of well-being as she went into the bath and turned on the water.

She stepped into beautifully tailored dark blue slacks and a thin cashmere sweater, brushed her hair vigorously, and eyed herself, unsmiling, her eyes bitter, before she turned to the door and let herself out into the hall.

She came into the kitchen, and Miss Bessie turned swiftly, startled.

"My, you're up early," she greeted the girl. "I was just about to bring your breakfast tray up."

"You mustn't wait on me, Miss Bessie," Brooke answered warmly. "I'm sure you have plenty to do taking trays to Uncle Ezra and Mr. Alden. Why can't I have breakfast and lunch here in the kitchen with you and Elijah?"

"Well, now, I'm not sure Mr. Ezra would approve."

"Oh, fiddle-faddle. What Mr. Ezra doesn't know surely won't hurt him. And I'm sure you have plenty to do without lugging trays upstairs. Ummm! That coffee smells good!"

"Mr. Ezra's real fond of my coffee," Miss Bessie admitted proudly. "How'll you have your eggs?"

"I won't, thanks," Brooke interposed hastily. "I don't eat breakfast — just coffee and orange juice. That is, if you have orange juice — "

"Sakes alive, yes — we have orange juice! Crates of oranges and grapefruit are shipped up from Florida every month! Mr. Ezra thinks citrus fruit is very healthy." Miss Bessie smiled at her, but added worriedly, "Juice and coffee's not much of a breakfast, Miss Brooke. I make very good French toast, if I do say so. Mr. Ezra says so, too."

"Thanks, Miss Bessie, I'm sure you do," Broke answered. "But I honestly don't want anything but a cup of coffee and a glass of orange juice."

The kitchen was big and warm and cheerful. There were red and white checked gingham curtains at the windows, and pots of red geraniums on the window sill above the sink. The floor was of red and black tiles, waxed to a gleaming lustre; the enormous refrigerator and the matching stove were snowy white, and the whole effect was very cheerful.

Seated at the small table beside the window, Brooke accepted the tall, frosty glass of orange juice Miss Bessie put before her and the cup of steaming, golden-brown coffee. There was a small jug of yellow cream, so thick it had to be spooned into the coffee.

Brooke said idly, "Robin Bryant gave me cream like this yesterday morning, and an enormous breakfast she called 'brunch' because it was late for breakfast and early for lunch. She's a darling, isn't she?"

"She is that," Miss Bessie agreed heartily, and added, "I worry about that child."

Brooke's eyebrows went up.

"For goodness sake, why? I've never seen a happier or more contented person — unless it's Kirke," she protested.

"That's why I worry about her." Miss Bessie poured herself a cup of coffee and joined Brooke at the table. "She's so devoted to Kirke that I'm afraid she'll miss having any life of her own. It would take a mighty fine boy to interest her — and after all, Robin's not getting any younger, you know."

Brooke paused, her coffee cup halfway to her mouth, her eyes widened.

"Why, Miss Bessie, she can't be more than eighteen!"

"She'll be nineteen this coming September," Miss Bessie said. "And up here girls marry young. Why, a lot of girls who are nineteen are already married and with babies! They marry at fifteen, or fourteen sometimes."

Brooke was shocked.

"Why, that's outrageous!" she gasped. "A child of fourteen and fifteen couldn't possibly know her own mind or if she was in love." She broke off and paled, her jaw tightening at the word.

"I'd hate to see Robin become one of those old maids that sacrifice everything for a bachelor brother," said Miss Bessie, pursuing the subject relentlessly. "Practically every unattached female in the whole county is after Kirke. One of 'em will trip him up one day, hog-tie him and drag him to the altar — and then where'll Robin be?"

Brooke said dryly, "You draw a pretty picture of marriage, Miss Bessie — 'trip him up, hog-tie him and drag him to the altar.' Are the unattached young women up here that predatory?"

Miss Bessie said with a frankness that Brooke found touching, "I don't know what the word 'predatory' means, Miss Brooke, but if it means do they go after a man like Kirke like he was some kind of wild game — I'm afraid they are. Aren't they like that everywhere?"

Brooke said grimly, "You could be right, Miss Bessie."

Miss Bessie nodded. "That's why I worry about Robin. If she'd date some of the young fellas that would like to take her around and that could marry her — " She sighed and stood up. "Well, after all, it's no skin off my nose, and I got no business worrying about her. But she's such a sweet, smart girl. I've known her since she was born, and I'm very fond of her."

"I think almost anybody would be,"

Brooke agreed as she, too, stood up and took her dishes to the sink. "Well, I'm going to clean my room, Miss Bessie."

"You'll do no such thing!" Miss Bessie protested, shocked.

In an unwonted show of affection, Brooke put her arm about the woman's wide, powerful shoulders and gave her a little hug.

"Look, Miss Bessie, I love it here, and I want to stay for as long as Uncle Ezra will let me, until I'm as old as he is, maybe!" she said firmly. "But only on condition that I don't add to your burden. Unless you let me take care of my own quarters and have my meals here with you and Elijah, and help any way I can — I'll pack up and leave immediately! You can take that as a threat or a promise, just as you choose!"

"Well, now," Miss Bessie was somewhat fussed, "since you put it like that, there's not much I can say, is there?"

"Yes," Brooke told her firmly. "You can say, 'well, now, if that's the way you want it'."

Miss Bessie laughed richly and warmly.

"Well, now, if that's the way you want it, Miss Brooke," she yielded. "But I bet you never made a bed or swept a floor or scrubbed a bathtub in your life!"

Brooke winced humorously.

"I'll have to say you're right," she admitted. "But I'll never learn any younger, will I?"

"Well, no, I reckon not," Miss Bessie agreed, and started as a bell above her head jangled sharply. "Oh, Mr. Ezra's ready for his morning coffee. I'll have to take it to him."

She turned to the stove and Brooke went up the stairs and to her own quarters.

When she had finished putting the rooms to rights, she examined the contents of her wardrobe. She had packed hastily on leaving New York.

It had never for a moment occurred to her that she would need formal evening wear, and so there was only the gray dress she had worn last night and a sheer pale green wool cocktail dress. That, she supposed Uncle Ezra would accept. He was such a darling that she wanted to do him proud and look her loveliest for him each evening.

She went down to lunch sometime later to find Elijah and Miss Bessie waiting for her. As she sat down at the table and unfolded her napkin, she realized that she was hungry. And the good, hearty smell of the food before her increased her appetite.

"It's just what I usually fix for Lije and me," Miss Bessie apologized anxiously. "I didn't know what to get out of the freezer for you. You'll have to tell me what you like."

"I like this," said Brooke hungrily, and helped herself to thick-sliced, still warm baked ham, green beans and carrots, tossed green salad, and eyed with warm appreciation the hot apple

81

pie Miss Bessie was removing from the oven.

"See, Maw?" said Elijah, with a wide grin. "I told you she was our kind of folks, even if she was a rich lady from up North."

Brooke laughed and patted his hand.

"I think that's one of the nicest compliments I ever received, Elijah. Thank you!" she said quite honestly.

"Shucks, you can call me Lije," he told her, smiling shyly. "Everybody does except Mr. Ezra, him being the formal type."

"He is, isn't he?" Brooke agreed, and smiled at Elijah in his overalls and stout boots and thick flannel shirt. "That's quite an act you put on at dinner last night, Lije. I'd have sworn you had been trained in some swanky English manor house."

"I was trained by Mr. Ezra, Miss Brooke, and believe you me, it was a rough training! Took me two-three months to get the hang of what he wanted me to do when I served at

82

the table. It's easy as falling off a log now. Do I do it good?"

"You do it perfect!" Brooke assured him solemnly. "Any time you want a job in New York, I can think of a dozen of my friends who'd jump at the chance to get you."

"Well, now, that's right kind of you, Miss Brooke. But I reckon Bessie and me'll just stay on here. We're mountain folk, born and bred, like our folks before us," Elijah answered earnestly. "Don't reckon me and her could stand living in the flatlands, or where there's a lot of people."

"You're very wise, Lije," Brooke told him gently.

"Not but what I'm plumb grateful to you, Miss Brooke," he assured her quickly. "It was right kind of you to make the offer."

"And it was right sensible of you to refuse it," Brooke told him.

After the meal was over, and Elijah had gone back outside, Brooke helped Miss Bessie, over her protests, do the dishes and clear away. As she finished, she asked, "Where could I find a telephone for a long distance call that's — well, private?"

Miss Bessie paused in her task of washing out the tea towels and said thoughtfully, "Well, now, the nearest telephone is at Miss Dovie's, about halfway down to town. But I reckon if you wanted it to be a real private call, you'd have to go all the way to town and call from the telephone exchange. That's about fifteen miles down the road, the way you came."

Brooke nodded. "I have to have some more clothes sent down," she confessed, smiling ruefully. "I didn't dream I'd need evening things and only brought the dress I wore last night. And it's really a cocktail or theatre dress. I have scads of them hanging up in closets at home, so it seems silly to shop for more. I thought I'd just telephone my housekeeper and ask her to pack a couple of bags and ship them down to me."

Miss Bessie nodded. "Now, that's a sensible thing to do. If she got them off tomorrow, you'd get 'em by the end of the week. That's if she saw to it they got off early tomorrow."

"She will," Brooke answered. "She's very reliable."

She hesitated for a moment, deep in thought, and then she smiled.

"I'd better run down there and put the call through," she decided. "And I think I'll stop and ask Robin to go with me."

"Oh, Robin would like that." Miss Bessie beamed happily.

"So would I," Brooke answered. "She's a darling."

7

ROBIN raced out to the car, her hair tousled, clad in ancient blue jeans and one of Kirke's shirts, and Brooke felt her heart warm to the girl as she led the way into the house.

"You've come for your coat and your suit, of course," Robin chattered. "I was going to bring it to you, but Kirke's using the jeep."

"Wait a minute." Brooke laughed and held the girl as she was about to hurry into the spare room. "I'd forgotten all about the silly coat."

Robin stared at her, rough-eyed.

"Forgotten it? A *mink* coat?" she gasped incredulously.

"I'm afraid I had," Brooke admitted, somewhat abashed at Robin's amazement. "I have to go down to the town, wherever it is, to make a telephone call, and I thought maybe you'd like to ride with me."

"Gollies!" Robin looked out of the window at the handsome, sleek car. "Would I ever just. Can you wait until I get slicked up a bit?"

"You look awfully cute as you are."

"Oh, but I couldn't go into town in pants!" Robin protested, and colored as she looked at Brooke's beautifully tailored slacks. "Oh, I would if they were like yours — I'd wear 'em to church on Sunday! But not old worn-out blue jeans. It won't take me long, if you're sure you don't mind waiting."

"I'm quite sure," Brooke told her lightly.

Robin scampered out of the room, and as she dressed, called back, "How do you like Peacock Hill? And Mr. Ezra?"

"I love it — and him! He's a darling." Brooke raised her voice so that it would carry to the other room. "That's why I have to make a phone call to my place in New York and have some more clothes sent down. I never dreamed they dressed for dinner at Peacock Hill."

"Do they really? Just Mr. Ezra and Mr. Tom?" Robin asked. "I've heard rumors about it, but I didn't know if it was true."

She came out of her room, looking young and scrubbed and very pretty in a brown skirt and sweater.

She looked at Brooke and then down at herself and flushed.

"I don't look much like a somebody that would be riding in a Cadillac like that one outside, do I?" she admitted ruefully.

"You look exactly like somebody any Cadillac would be proud to transport," Brooke said firmly. "Why don't you wear the mink coat, since you like it so much?"

"Oh, I wouldn't dare."

"Why not? I'd be glad to have you keep it for yourself, if you will accept it," Brooke answered.

Robin's head went up and her blue

eyes chilled slightly.

"Thank you, but I couldn't possibly accept it," she said coldly.

Puzzled, Brooke asked, "Well, for heaven's sake, why not? If I want to give it you and you like it — "

"I couldn't possibly accept it," Robin repeated stubbornly. "Besides, where would I wear it? Out to feed the chickens, or to go fishing?"

"You've just said you go to church."

"Kirke wouldn't let me have it, and I wouldn't take it anyway, but thanks a whole lot just the same." Robin was still stiff and cold-eyed.

Brooke studied her for a moment, frowning slightly. "Robin, if you so much as *think* the word 'charity', I'll slap you," she threatened.

For a moment the two girls eyed each other, and suddenly a bubble of mirth escaped Robin, and her eyes danced.

"You know something? I bet you would, too," she gurgled, and the momentary tension was dissolved. "And

I hadn't even thought of the word charity."

"I'm glad to hear that," Brooke informed her sharply. "For a minute there you looked as if you were about to say something I'd *have* to slap you for."

"Well, I wasn't," Robin said cheerfully. "Shall we get started? I'll have to be back in time to get Kirke's supper. He'll be good and hungry when he gets back."

She led the way out of the house, pulled the door shut and started toward the car.

"Aren't you going to leave a note for him to tell him where you are?" asked Brooke.

"Golly, no. He'll think I've gone fishing," Robin laughed.

"But you forgot to lock the door."

Robin looked honestly astonished.

"Golly, nobody locks doors up here," she protested. "If neighbors stop by for something they need and find the door locked, they're insulted."

Brooke sighed and shook her head.

"This is a perfectly fantastic place," she said as she slid beneath the wheel of the big car.

They came to the turn-off where she and Kirke had parked the day before. Beyond it the road dropped steeply, so steeply that Brooke was startled.

"I don't remember driving along this road," she said.

"You were driving straight up," Robin pointed out. "It's when you start down that it looks so scary."

Covertly she watched Brooke's taut face as the car slid and twisted down the steep grade, and understood the emotions that were tugging at Brooke's consciousness. She began to chatter casually, her intent to take Brooke's mind off the road; but Brooke gave her only token attention, so absorbed was she in the perilous road.

As they came down a few miles from the turn-off, a small dilapidated shack of a building, weathered by many years, clung precariously to the side of the mountain that had been scooped out at the back to hold it. Above it a sign read: "General Store: Dovie Grayson." Seated on the narrow front porch in an old-fashioned rocker was an enormous woman in a faded calico dress, a sunbonnet on her head, placidly smoking a corncob pipe. She waved as the car slid past, and Brooke risked taking an eye from the road to glance at Robin.

"I don't believe it," she said firmly.

"Don't believe what?"

"That woman was smoking a corncob pipe!"

"Miss Dovie? Well, sure she was. Why not? And she was smoking chewing tobacco that she shaves off a plug."

"Robin, that's why I don't believe it! It's something people just imagine when they think of hillbillies."

"That's a dirty word in these parts," Robin said with mock sternness, a twinkle in her eyes. "We're mountain folk, not hillbillies!"

"I didn't mean you and Kirke, or even Miss Bessie and Elijah," Brooke protested. "I meant people like that old woman."

"Well, don't let Miss Dovie hear you say it," Robin warned. "She'll cut you down to size! Poor Miss Dovie!"

"Why 'poor Miss Dovie'? She looked very comfortable and very satisfied." Brooke's attention was chiefly on the road, and the lower they descended along its narrow twisted length the more appalled she became.

"Oh, Miss Dovie was devoted to her brother, Claude," said Robin. "Claude was three years younger than she, and what's politely called up here 'not quite right in the head.' But she worshipped him, and when he died a few years ago, Miss Dovie just about went to pieces. She wouldn't leave that place; said Claude was still there and she couldn't go off and leave him. She talks to him even when people are in the store and behaves just as if he were there. She told me herself she always sets two places at the table, because though she knows he won't eat, she doesn't want to hurt his feelings by not showing him he'd be welcome."

"Robin, I don't believe a word of that," Brooke protested, and caught her breath as the car skidded ever so slightly on a turn that was too sharp. "The next thing you'll be telling me Peacock Hill is haunted."

Robin laughed and said, "Well, of course Peacock Hill is haunted. Hasn't Miss Bessie told you?"

"Haunted, I suppose, by the moaning of slaves long dead and the creaking of chains and doors opening and shutting when there's no one there?" Brooke's tone was scornful.

"Oh, golly, no!" Robin assured her cheerfully. "It's haunted by the scream of the white peacocks that used to live there. Folks say that at midnight on nights when the moon is a quarter full, you can hear them screaming and screeching. Folks up and down the mountain have heard them, but nobody has seen them."

The road made one final sharp curve, and they came out in the floor of the valley. Brooke gave a gasp of sheer pleasure, pulled the car up and stopped. She glanced back at the road they had descended, shuddered and for a moment put her hands over her face.

Robin looked about her uneasily. The road was little more than a narrow ledge beside a swiftly flowing stream. On either side the mountains rose steeply. The river foughts its way between huge black rocks, that churned its swift-rushing waters into white foam, and the whole narrow, deep valley was alive with its noise.

"Please, Brooke," Robin said suddenly, "let's not stop here. Harmony Grove is just a mile ahead. I hate this spot more than any spot I've ever known in all my life! It's why I hate to come down to Harmony Grove, because you have to drive through here."

Brooke started the car and looked curiously at Robin, noting the pallor of the cute, piquant face and the eyes that searched this way and that as though fearful of some evil that might at any moment leap out of the shrubbery or the rocks.

"Why, Robin, what's wrong with the place?" she asked. "And don't give me any more of that idiotic guff about ghosts."

"Oh, it's nothing like that," Robin assured her earnestly. "It's just that I hate feeling hemmed in, as if the mountains could sneeze and drop in on top of me."

Brooke looked startled as she followed the direction of the girl's eyes toward the mountain that rose on the left, without so much as the faintest semblance of a trail or anything human. On the right, across the narrow, brawling river, another mountain seemed to shoot up as though trying to reach the sky.

"Why, honey — " she began gently,

as she started the car up again.

"Don't bother telling me how silly it is, because I know," Robin said grimly, eyes straight ahead, hands locked tightly in her lap. "You know that line in the Twenty-Third Psalm — 'Though I walk through the valley of the shadow of death'? Well, to me this *is* the valley of the shadow of death, and it scares me simple!"

"You should have known some of my thoughts as we were falling down that awful road, expecting to meet another car at any minute and knowing there wouldn't be an inch of room to pass," Brooke confessed.

The little town seemed to sleep peacefully beneath the frail March sunshine, and to Brooke it appeared a pleasant place with tree-shaded streets, neat white houses set back behind picket fences or old weathered gray houses. There was a 'business block,' most of the buildings old and weathered and with commodious verandahs where a few elderly men sat and hound dogs slept peacefully. There were also a dozen or more modern-looking places, some of them even showing neon lights.

"Now where would the telephone exchange be?" suggested Brooke, as they came slowly into town.

"There's a telephone in the drugstore," offered Robin.

"With a booth?"

"Goodness, no!"

"Miss Bessie thought I'd have a better chance of a private call if I made it directly from the telephone exchange."

"Miss Bessie is so right," Robin agreed, and directed her to a small brick building set back from the street, with the familiar sign on a brass plaque attached to its wall.

Brooke parked the car and got out.

"I won't be long, Robin."

Robin chuckled and slid out of the car.

"If you want to make a private call, Brooke my fran'," she mocked, "you'd better let me go in with you

98

and hold conversation with Miss Elvie while you talk."

Brooke's eyebrows went up.

"You don't mean she'd listen in?"

"Well, now, I ask you," said Robin reasonably, "if you spent your whole life in a place like Harmony Grove, and somebody wanted to make a long distance call to New York, wouldn't you be mildly interested?"

"I see what you mean," Brooke admitted ruefully.

"You could have called from Miss Dovie's," Robin explained. "Her's is the last telephone up the mountain until you get over on the other side, beyond Peacock Hill. Kirke and I felt it was an unnecessary expense to have it come to our place; and Mr. Ezra all but had conniptions when the telephone people suggested installing one for him. Miss Dovie is on a party line — an eight-party line!"

She laughed at Brooke's expression as they went into the trim, neat little building.

A tall, thin woman in her early forties stood behind the desk, and a girl sat at the switchboard. The thin woman came forward, greeting Robin eagerly, smiling tentatively at Brooke.

"Well, hello, Robin. Long time no see," said the thin woman.

"Ain't it the truth?" Robin agreed cheerfully. "Miss Elvie, this is Mrs. Hildreth. She's visiting at Peacock Hill, and she wants to place a New York call."

"Howdy do, Mrs. Hildreth?" said Miss Elvie happily. "We'll be glad to put the call through. To whom is it going, and do you know the number, and is it a station-to-station or a person-to-person?"

Brooke supplied the number and said, "Person to person, please. I want to speak to Mr. Layne Meredith, no one else in the office. If he's gone for the day, I'll try his home."

Miss Elvie nodded and went off briskly to the girl at the switchboard, who accepted the slip of paper, glanced curiously at Brooke, smilingly at Robin and began placing the call.

Brooke heard her saying importantly, "Hello, New York? Connect me with Murray Hill." She looked down at the slip and read the number off very carefully.

There was a small delay, and then the girl nodded to Miss Elvie, who said importantly, "Here's your party, Mrs. Hildreth. You can take the call in the booth over there."

Brooke thanked her, crossed to the booth and drew the door shut behind her.

8

BROOKE lifted the receiver, and a man's voice said impatiently, "Hello? Hello?"

Brooke said quietly, "Hello, Layne."

"Brooke!" She heard his startled gasp. "They said Mrs. Hildreth was calling from some weird place in North Carolina — I couldn't believe it. What in the name of all that's logical are you doing there?"

"I'm visiting my uncle, Layne," Brooke told him.

"Your uncle lives in North Carolina? Brooke, I didn't even know you *had* an uncle. Brooke, are you all right?" Layne's words rushed together. "I've been worried stiff about you, just dropping out of sight like that without a word to anybody. I heard you'd gone to Cap d'Antibes to visit your mother — and a more unlikely story I couldn't imagine."

"Neither can I," Brooke answered. "Layne, I want you to do something for me — "

"Name it, Brooke, and consider it done."

"I want you to get my housekeeper to pack a lot of evening clothes for me and ship them here the fastest possible way."

"Evening clothes?" he gasped incredulously.

"You know, darling." Brooke laughed at his astonishment. "Formal gowns, with all the accessories — the sort of thing I always put on when I went dining and dancing with you."

"But, Brooke, what in blazes would you do with that kind of clothes in a place called — what is it the girl said? — Harmony Grove?"

"Oh, we're very formal down here," Brooke mocked him lightly. "We dress for dinner every night! I can't afford to be seen in the same thing every night, and I only brought two 'dress-for-dinner' formals. So will you, Layne?"

"You know I will," Layne assured her. "I'll go right over to your apartment and see to it. I'll get the stuff off tonight — first thing tomorrow if it's too late to catch the next train south. I don't suppose air-mail would help? I mean, *is* there an airport at Harmony Grove?"

"I'm afraid not; the nearest airport is at Asheville," Brooke assured him. "Just send things by express. It shouldn't take more than a few days, and I'll manage with the two I have until then. How have *you* been, Layne?"

"Aside from worrying about you — "

"You mustn't, Layne. I'm all right, really I am!" she told him swiftly. "I'll see you one of these days."

"That'll be something to look forward to," said Layne, and hung up the receiver.

She drew a deep breath, pulled the door of the booth open and went outside, where Miss Elvie and Robin were chattering away happily.

"Did you have a good connection?"

104

asked Miss Elvie.

"Oh, yes, splendid, thank you," Brooke answered, and opened her wallet to pay the charges. "I got through right away, much faster than I had dared hope."

"Oh, we pride ourselves on good service," Miss Elvie told her. "You should try to persuade Mr. Calloway to have a phone installed. It would save you that drive."

"Oh, I doubt I shall be here long enough for that, and I wouldn't think of trying to interfere with his way of living," Brooke assured her.

"Oh, I was hoping you'd be here all summer," said Miss Elvie. "You must bring her to church Sunday, Robin. And the square dance Saturday might be a novelty for her. I hope you and Kirke are planning to be here?"

"I really don't know, Miss Elvie," Robin answered. "Kirke hasn't decided yet. But we'll be seeing you soon."

Robin nodded, and with a hand

under Brooke's elbow urged her out into the sunshine, where Robin gave a small gurgling laugh.

"Poor Miss Elvie! She never gives up," she murmured as though to herself.

Brooke eyed her curiously.

"Poor Miss Elvie? Don't tell me she's grieving for a lost brother?" she mocked.

"Not that one!" Robin answered cheerfully. "She's pursuing my brother, who isn't a bit lost, except where she's concerned."

Brooke stared, as they reached the car.

"That desiccated old maid is pursuing Kirke?" She was frankly shocked.

"Don't worry — she's not going to get him! Kirke's much too fast on his feet — and much too wary." Robin laughed. "And there's me to contend with, too. Kirke's my favorite brother. I'm not turning him over to the likes of Miss Elvie, I can assure you."

106

"Well, I should hope not. Why, she must be ten years older than Kirke," Brooke protested.

Robin chuckled. "If you want to be really charitable," she agreed. "Kirke's twenty-six."

Brooke looked swiftly at Robin, and they both laughed. It was Robin who sobered first.

"I'm not making fun of Miss Elvie," she insisted. "She's a good, kind creature who's devoted her whole life to looking after an aged mother, who died about a year ago. And Miss Elvie is lost without something or somebody to take care of. I guess she needs to be needed. And that's pretty important, isn't it?"

Brooke's mouth had a bitter twist.

"I should imagine so," she agreed, and added quickly, "Well, what's next?"

"Let's have a drink," suggested Robin eagerly, "to give us strength for that drive home."

"A drink?" Brooke repeated, startled.

"I always feel it's illegal to come to Harmony Grove and not have a drink and browse in the dime store," Robin told her cheerfully, leading the way along the sidewalk.

They entered a drugstore, clean, immaculate, with a big soda fountain and bright-colored seats with booths. It was mid-afternoon. Most of the booths were occupied, and there were half a dozen teenagers along the fountain.

It seemed to Brooke that Robin knew them all and there was a friendly hubbub of greetings, as Robin led the way to the front booth where two gangling teenage boys lounged over magazines taken from the racks.

"On your feet, Bub," Robin greeted them sternly. "Make way for the cash customers."

"Oh, hi, Robbie." The boys grinned, without offense, and vacated the booth, eyeing Brooke with shy but lively interest.

Before she sat down, Robin signaled

to the soda-fountain man, in a white coat and cap gaily aslant over one ear.

"The usual, Bennie, my boy," she called. "Make it snappy."

"Coming up, Robbie," Bennie answered, and a moment later came carrying a tray on which were two enormous chocolate sodas.

"Two scoops of ice cream?" demanded Robin suspiciously.

"Would I offer you less?" protested Bennie, hurt.

"You'd better not," she threatened him darkly, and grinned impishly. "Brooke, this is Bennie Farland, who used to be a pal of mine when I was a callow school-gal. Bennie, this is my friend, Mrs. Hildreth."

"Happy to meet you, ma'am," said Bennie, and hurried back to his duties behind the fountain.

Brooke looked at the two chocolate sodas, tipped back her head and laughed.

Robin, dipping a spoon in the ice

cream, looked up at her, puzzled.

"Oh, come now, we're not all *that* funny in Harmony Grove," she protested.

"I'm laughing at *me*, Robin, not at you," Brooke confessed. "You said, 'Let's have a drink' — and I swear I thought you meant a cocktail, at the very least. To have twin chocolate sodas placed in front of us instead — well, somehow it struck me as very funny, in the light of what I was expecting."

Wide-eyed, Robin gasped, "Gollies! Did you think I was going to lead you into some dim-lit sink of iniquity and ply you with hard likker?"

"Well, after all, you *did* say a drink," Brooke defended herself.

By now the youngsters in the drugstore had recovered from their awe of the stranger, Brooke, and were clustered about the booth, laughing, chattering in what seemed to Brooke completely unintelligible gibberish.

A tall, sandy haired boy who wore

skin-tight levis and a T-shirt bent above Robin.

"Hi, Robin, how about dragging you to the hop Saturday?" he asked anxiously.

Robin looked up at him, laughing.

"As if you didn't know as well as I do that heap of yours would die halfway up the mountain!" she mocked.

"Well, sure, I know that, but if you come down with Kirke, I'll promise to swing you high, wide and handsome," the boy insisted.

"I don't know yet whether we'll be down or not," Robin answered.

"You've never missed a shag before," the boy insisted.

"Well, then it's about time I did, don't you think?"

"But, Robbie, this is going to be something special," the boy pleaded. "We've got Mr. Dacey and his Jug Band, and you know he's the best caller in the country. And the music is loud and free!"

"Sounds good," Robin told him casually. "I'll see how Kirke feels about it."

The boy turned to Brooke.

"I hope you'll come too, ma'am," he said politely.

"Thank you," said Brooke, slightly dazed at being called 'ma'am.'

A stout, white-coated man with thin gray hair came over, and the youngsters moved politely out of his way.

"Hello, Robbie, it's nice to see you down this way," he greeted Robin.

"Hello, Doc, it's nice to be here," said Robin politely. "Brooke, this is Dr. Newsom. My friend Mrs. Hildreth, Doc. She's visiting at Peacock Hill."

"Indeed," said Dr. Newsom, and looked interested. "I've heard some fascinating stories about the old place. Never had the pleasure of meeting either Mr. Calloway or Mr. Alden. I understand they drive down the other side of the mountain and on to Asheville. It's only about forty miles that way."

"I'm afraid I wouldn't know about that," Brooke answered politely. "I've only been here a few days."

"I hope you'll stay all summer," Dr. Newsom urged pleasantly, "and that you will come to the Grove again with Robbie. We miss her here, now that she's finished high school. Used to see a lot of her while she was living with her aunt. How's Miss Grace getting along, Robbie?"

"Oh, she loves it with her sister in Asheville," answered Robin. "She was so glad to be able to sell her house here and go to Ashville, after Kirke came home. She would have been pretty lonely after I finished school."

"Yes, I suppose so," Dr. Newsom agreed. "We hated to give her up, though. She was a sort of leading spirit in all the worth-while things here-about."

Robin nodded, a twinkle in her eyes. "A one-woman Chamber of Commerce, wasn't she?" she agreed. "She had what's politely known as a lot of drive, didn't she?"

Dr. Newsom grinned at the twinkle. "Well, let's say she got things done," he answered. "I hear another of those roadhouses is re-opening. They were all closed while Miss Grace was here."

"They were indeed," murmured Robin. "All Aunt Grace had to do was drive out, have a talk with the operators and if she didn't like what she saw — bingo! The joint was shut!"

"Well, I can't say I don't think it was a vast improvement," Dr. Newsom said a trifle stiffly. "We're really going to miss her when the summer folks begin to arrive."

"I'm sure you will," Robin answered, and looked at Brooke. "If we're going to get home before dark, hadn't we better get started?"

Brooke shuddered and stood up.

"There are many things I can think of that I'd like better than being caught on that road after dark," she admitted. "I wouldn't want it to happen twice."

She nodded goodbye to Dr. Newsom,

assured him she would be in again, and Robin made her way out through the clamorous friends who seemed loath to let her go. Robin stepped grandly into the Cadillac, and Brooke slid beneath the wheel.

"You have a lot of friends, Robin," said Brooke enviously.

"Don't you?" asked Robin curiously.

Brooke's mouth tightened, and she made no answer as the big car slid away from the curb and headed toward the road out of town.

9

THE jeep was parked near the house, and as the Cadillac rolled down the drive, Kirke came out to meet them, his momentary anxiety fading as he saw them together.

"I was about to get out a posse to hunt you, Small Fry," he told Robin when he had greeted Brooke. "I thought you'd gone fishing and probably fallen in the creek!"

"Thanks," Robin laughed. "As if I couldn't swim!"

She turned eagerly to Brooke.

"Stay and have supper with us," she urged.

"I've got it almost ready for the table," Kirke added, smiling. "And if I do say so, I'm a pretty fair cook."

"He's the best," Robin boasted.

"Don't tempt me," Brooke smiled warmly from one to the other. "I'd love it. But I'm afraid it would be rude to Uncle Ezra. He *does* seem pleased I'm here."

"You sound surprised! Why shouldn't he be?" Robin demanded.

Brooke smiled at her and then at Kirke.

"I like your little sister," she said lightly.

"Oh, she'll do, in a pinch," Kirke answered, his tone making the words a paean of praise as he reached out and rumpled Robin's black curls.

"Isn't she a darling, Kirke?" Robin laughed up at him and then turned to Brooke. "How about going to the dance with us Saturday?"

"Oh," asked Kirke, "are we going?"

"Well, you don't want to break Miss Elvie's heart, do you?" Robin countered briskly.

Kirke gave her a stern glance.

"Nor the hearts of half a dozen callow teenagers who'll be swarming around you like bees around a hive," he reminded her.

"Brooke will go along to protect you from Miss Elvie," promised Robin gaily.

"And who's going to protect you from all the Bills and Jerries and Martins and Coys?" demanded Kirke.

"Oh, pish!" said Robin airily. "I can handle them."

"You know something?" asked Brooke. "She can, too. I watched her this afternoon — the girl is good! The way she wraps them around her little finger, then just casually brushes them aside and makes them love it is fantastic."

"Oh, it takes talent," Robin said modestly.

"Sure you won't stay for supper?" Kirke urged.

"I'm sure. Thanks a lot. Maybe some other time. I'll have to hurry back to Peacock Hill if I'm going to be dressed for dinner by seven and not keep Uncle Ezra waiting," Brooke answered. "Miss Bessie seems to think he might do something drastic if dinner was late — and I'm not aiming to find out!"

"We'll see you Saturday then," Robin called. "And don't be afraid of the road — Kirke will drive."

"In that case, then, it's a date," Brooke said, and drove off.

Kirke looked down curiously at Robin's entranced young face and said quietly, "You had fun I take it?"

"Oh, such grand fun! She's such a darling." Robin glowed.

She went into the kitchen and sniffed delightedly. "Oh, Kirke, you made Italian spaghetti."

"Don't I always when I cook?" He chuckled.

"No, you cook lots of fancy things that I wouldn't know how to start making. My favorite is Italian spaghetti. I'll make a salad."

"It's made, and the Greek dressing, too," Kirke assured her. "I thought you'd be all tired out from tussling with a fish or two — "

"I'll go fishing tomorrow afternoon, I promise you." She laughed. "I bet I can catch Old Granddad if I try hard enough."

"Don't try! From the tales I hear about him, I'm not at all sure he's a monster catfish; I think he must be an alligator," Kirke warned her, only half-joking. "I mean it, Small Fry. If something lifts its head and looks more like a bulldog than a fish, leave it be — you hear me?"

"I hear, Master. Your wish is my command!" she mocked him, and held out her hand for the heaping plate of spaghetti he was holding across the table to her.

Brooke drove to Peacock Hill and went in through the kitchen, where Miss Bessie turned from dinner preparation and glanced swiftly at the clock.

"You'll have to hurry, Miss Brooke. It's twenty minutes to seven," she warned. Brooke nodded and raced upstairs.

She came down as the big old grandfather clock gave forth its seven mellow 'bongs'. Elijah, loitering in the hall, out of sight of the living room, held up his fingers in the familiar 'O' sign that means all is well. Brooke winked at him and went into the living room, where Ezra and Tom were just finishing their before-dinner cocktails.

"Oh, there you are, my dear," said Ezra as though genuinely glad to see her. "Tom and I had begun to believe you'd run away."

"Oh, goodness, no, Uncle Ezra." Brooke laughed and impulsively dropped a light kiss on his cheek. "You won't get rid of me that easily. Robin and I went into town."

Behind her Elijah said solemnly, "Dinner is served."

Ezra rose and offered Brooke his arm, smiling at her. "You and Robin went to Asheville?" he asked as they walked into the dining room and Elijah held her chair.

"Oh, goodness, no." Brooke smiled her thanks over her shoulder at Elijah. "We drove down to that little town in the valley where Robin lived and went to school while her brother was abroad. Harmony Grove, they call it."

"That brute of a road!" Tom said.

"It is, isn't it?" Brooke agreed. "I came that way the night I arrived, but it was so dark and storming so hard I had no idea it was so bad. Of course, as Robin pointed out, it's much easier to climb straight up than it is to drive down it."

"You should have taken the road I take, Brooke, to Asheville," Tom pointed out. "It's much better traveling; not so steep nor so winding."

"So Robin told me later," Brooke said. "I wanted to put a long distance telephone call through, and she said there was an exchange in Harmony Grove, and it's only fifteen miles or so."

Ezra paused in his enjoyment of his soup.

"I suppose, Tom, we really *should* have a telephone installed," he said reluctantly.

"Not just because I'm here, Uncle

Ezra. Don't you even think of such a thing," Brooke protested warmly. "When I have occasion to telephone, I can call from Miss Dovie's. And I hardly think I'll have any further use for a phone. I called a friend in New York and asked him to have my housekeeper send me some more clothes."

She looked from one to the other and smiled.

"That should be fair warning to you that I'm going to be the 'man who came to dinner' — and stayed and stayed and stayed! You'll probably have to have Elijah set my luggage on the doorstep and order me off the premises!"

Ezra smiled warmly at her.

"If you wait for that to happen, my dear, I'm afraid you'll be here a long, long time," he told her. "We hope so, don't we, Tom?"

"You're sweet, Uncle Ezra," said Brooke, and there was a faint huskiness in her voice. "When I think of the way

I just barged in on you when you didn't even know you had a niece, I'm ashamed of myself."

"You are at home, my dear," Ezra told her gently. "I'm very happy you thought of me and wanted to visit me. And we'll keep you just as long as you can be happy here."

"Thank you, darling." Brooke smiled at him, misty-eyed. "I know how you hate having your privacy invaded."

"I'm beginning to wonder if maybe we aren't wrong to make such recluses of ourselves, Tom." Ezra smiled across the table at his companion and friend. "If we could always guarantee that our privacy would be invaded by such a lovely lady, maybe we should arrange to be invaded more often."

"It's an intriguing thought, Ezra," Tom agreed. "But I doubt if we could get such a guarantee."

"Robin and Kirke have invited me to a dance Saturday night, a square dance," she said lightly, setting herself to be as entertaining and as pleasant a guest as she could. "Do you think I'd like it? I've never been to a square dance. I'm not sure I know just what is meant."

"It's a native folk dance," Ezra explained, "brought over by the early settlers, as I understand it. It's a rather wild, romping sort of dance, isn't it, Tom?"

Tom laughed deprecatingly. "I'm afraid I wouldn't know, Ezra," he admitted. "The Waltz and the minuet are more in my line, I'm afraid."

"Oh, come now," protested Brooke laughing, "I'll bet you are a wonderful dancer."

"It's been so long since I've tried — " Tom said.

"Mrs. Thrailkill and Elijah should be able to describe it to you." Ezra smiled. "I'm sure you will enjoy it."

Friday evening as she and the two gentle, courtly old men were having coffee in the big drawing room, there was the sound of a car in the drive, the slam of a car door and then a brisk rat-a-tat at the front door.

Startled, Ezra put down his fragile coffee cup and his white, bushy brows drew together in a startled frown.

"Who in the world can that be?" he wondered as Elijah went forward to answer the summons.

There was the murmur of voices, and then Elijah, looking startled, appeared in the doorway, saying, "A gentleman asking for Mrs. Hildreth, sir."

Before Brooke could do more than rise, as startled as the others, a man stood behind Elijah, and Brooke cried out sharply, "Layne Meredith! What in the world are you doing here?"

Layne brushed past Elijah, looking quickly about the room. Tall, suntanned, blond and blue-eyed, he was a disturbingly young and handsome intruder into the scene.

"I brought your luggage," he told Brooke, his eyes begging her to accept his arrival with pleasure.

"But, Layne dear, I didn't dream you'd bring it; I only asked you to send it," Brooke protested, and turned to Ezra. "Uncle Ezra, may I introduce a very good friend, Layne Meredith? Layne, this is my uncle, Ezra Calloway, and Mr. Alden."

Ezra greeted Layne with pleasant, friendly warmth.

"Welcome to Peacock Hill, sir." He shook hands firmly. "It's a pleasure to welcome a friend of my niece."

"Thank you, sir, that's very kind of you," Layne answered, and shook hands with Tom.

"Have you had dinner, Mr. Meredith?" asked Ezra while Brooke could do little more than stare at him, not quite willing to believe that he was really there.

"Yes, sir, thanks. I had dinner at Harmony Grove," answered Layne. And to Brooke, his tone taking on a faint hint of defensiveness, "I *had* to talk to you, Brooke."

"If you dined in Harmony Grove, Mr. Meredith," Ezra smiled at him, "I'm afraid you didn't dine very well. Elijah, could Mrs. Thrailkill find something for Mr. Meredith to eat?"

"Oh, sure. I mean, of course, sir," Elijah answered quickly, and hurried kitchen-ward.

"Oh, but you mustn't bother, sir," Layne protested. "I'll just leave Brooke's luggage and find a hotel and come back to see her tomorrow."

"A hotel? In Harmony Grove?" Tom laughed and shook his head. "I'm quite sure, Mr. Meredith, that the nearest hotel is in the opposite direction, at Asheville. And that's forty miles."

"So you will stay here, Mr. Meredith, at Peacock Hill," Ezra told him firmly.

"Oh, but I couldn't impose, Mr. Calloway — "

"Nonsense, Mr. Meredith. I believe we have an ample supply of rooms, haven't we, Brooke my dear?" Ezra protested.

"Goodness, yes," Brooke answered, "scads of them. But after all, Uncle Ezra — "

"After all, my dear, he is your good friend, and this is your home, and he is most welcome."

"That's very kind of you, sir," Layne answered. It was obvious that he was somewhat dazed and bewildered by the whole set-up; he turned accusingly to Brooke. "When you run away and lose yourself, you really do a fine job of it, don't you? If you hadn't mentioned over the telephone that you were with your uncle at a place called Peacock Hill, and the telephone operator hadn't said, 'Harmony Grove, North Carolina, calling,' I'd never have found you! Of course, when I asked at a filling station in the village for a place called Peacock Hill where a Mr. Ezra Calloway lived, the man told me it was fifteen miles. What he didn't tell me was that it was fifteen miles straight up. What a road!" he shuddered and turned swiftly to Ezra with a note of apology. "I'm sorry, sir. I suppose you're used to it."

Ezra laughed. "I have never been

over the road, Mr. Meredith, in the ten years I've lived here."

"Oh," said Layne, understanding. "Then there *is* another road. I felt sure there must be."

"Not from Harmony Grove, I'm afraid," Ezra answered, a twinkle in his eyes. "Tom, I believe, drives to Asheville over a road in the opposite direction. It's better, isn't it, Tom?"

"It would have to be," Layne answered as Tom nodded. "It couldn't be any worse, not if they expect cars to travel it."

Elijah appeared in the doorway.

"Dinner is ready, Mr. Meredith," he announced.

"Come along, Layne," said Brooke firmly, and took his arm and smiled at Ezra and Tom. "You will excuse us, won't you?"

She guided him to the dining room and there turned sharply on him.

"Layne, you needn't have come here — "

Layne's jaw set hard.

"Oh, yes, I needed to, Brooke," he said grimly. "You've run away long enough. There are things you have to face up to, and now's the time."

Brooke went a little pale.

"You mean, of course, that Julie is making trouble?"

"I mean that you have to get things settled, Brooke, and bring this whole miserable mess to a close."

The swinging door from the kitchen quarters swung open, and Miss Bessie came in, bearing a laden tray. Elijah had already set a place at the table, and Miss Bessie smiled at Layne as she arranged the food.

"I'm right sorry, Mr. Meredith, that there wasn't time to thaw a steak for you," she explained. "And I'm ashamed to offer you leftover from dinner. But it'll hold body and soul together until breakfast."

"You're very kind — " Layne began.

"Miss Bessie, this is my friend Layne Meredith from New York," said Brooke, and added to Layne,

131

"and, Layne, this is Miss Bessie — Mrs. Thrailkill — my friend at Peacock Hill."

Layne smiled and held out his hand.

"Hello, Miss Bessie. I'm glad she has such a nice friend here."

Miss Bessie shook hands heartily, liking the tall, blue-eyed man with his thick, close-cropped hair that was the color of wheat straw.

"And I'm mighty glad she has a friend from New York to visit her, so maybe she'll stay all summer," she answered. "Elijah's fixing a room for you, Mr. Meredith, and carrying the luggage up from the car."

"Oh, but he needn't do that. I'm not staying. I only came to bring Brooke some things," Layne began.

Miss Bessie laughed richly.

"Right cold to spend the night on the mountain, Mr. Meredith," she told him. "And this is about the only place between here and Asheville for you to stay. I wouldn't want to drive either the road to Harmony Grove or the one to Asheville this late at night, this time of year. You set now and eat your dinner before it gets cold."

She walked out without giving him a chance to answer, and Layne looked helplessly at Brooke, who was grinning ruefully.

"You'd better do as she says," she warned him. "Miss Bessie is a bit of a martinet, as well as a fantastically good cook."

He took his place at the table, and she sat opposite him as he dug an experimental fork into the dish before him.

"Hi, that's good," he said, and added quickly, anxiously, "Brooke, are you angry with me because I came?"

"It's not that, Layne," she answered awkwardly, trying to decide just what it was that had made her so unwilling to see him. "It's just that I don't want to talk about that any more."

"But, Brooke baby — "

"Don't call me 'Baby'!" she flashed

at him so hotly that he looked startled and then angry.

"Sorry, it *was* David's pet name for you, wasn't it?" he said through his teeth. For a moment they glared at each other, and it was Layne who looked away first. "That was a blow beneath the belt, for which I'm sorry."

Brooke drew a deep hard breath, and her hand clenched tightly.

"I told you, the last time I saw you in New York, that Julie could have the money, all of it. I didn't want a penny," she said through her teeth.

"But that wasn't the way David wanted it."

"How could you possibly know what David wanted?" she flashed.

Layne studied her for a moment, his jaw set.

"I probably knew what he wanted a lot better than you did," he stated flatly.

"That could easily be," she answered tautly, "because I only *thought* I knew what he wanted — and was I ever wrong! I thought he wanted *me* — and all the time it was Julie."

"Not all the time, Brooke," Layne told her earnestly. "Only the last few weeks, when you were so busy with the preparations for the wedding that he felt neglected, and Julie was available — "

"Very available," Brooke answered, tight-lipped. "And David didn't have the guts to tell me." Her voice broke and she set her teeth hard, blinking against the shameful tears.

"David had never had much experience in facing unpleasant things," Layne said.

"Like telling a girl he was marrying her for her money and wanted an immediate divorce as soon as the wedding was over?" Brooke asked tautly.

"He didn't really mean that."

"Oh, be quiet!" Brooke flashed at him furiously. "He told me so himself — an hour after the ceremony — just before we started on our honeymoon to

Paris, where a divorce would be easy."

"Brooke, darling, believe me, he would never have gone through with it! He'd have forgotten Julie."

"And I was supposed to fight for my man?" she said through her teeth, her tone making the cliché insulting. "Well, I didn't want him — when I knew the truth."

She jerked to her feet, her eyes stormy.

"I told you, Layne, when I left New York, I didn't want to talk about it, and I still don't," she told him, her voice shaking. "I won't talk about it. You knew him better than I did. You'd been friends since college days. You'd known me since childhood. You introduced us — remember?"

"And he took you away from me," said Layne quietly, and added, with a smile that was little more than a grimace, "You really can't lose something you've never had, can you? And since you never knew that I loved you —"

136

Brooke stared at him, wide-eyed, incredulous.

"Why, Layne, you never told me — "

"I know, so I deserved to lose you, and I did," he said grimly. "I was waiting until I had something to offer you. And before I could get there, you'd met David and that was that."

Brooke was staring at him.

"Layne, I never dreamed you were in love with me," she said.

"*Am*, not *was*," he corrected her quietly.

"And you knew all along about Julie and David — and yet you never warned me?" her voice was low and shaken.

"Would it have done any good? You'd have thought it was my jealousy speaking. And it would have been, partially, I admit. You wouldn't have believed that David was serious about Julie. I don't believe he was."

"Oh, don't you?"

Layne shook his head, his eyes holding hers steadily. "I never will believe it," he told her grimly. "That's why I won't turn over his estate to her as you're asking me to do."

"Well, I believe it," Brooke said stormily. "I couldn't not believe it after that awful scene after the wedding — just before he rushed out and and into his car and — crashed."

She put her face in her hands for a moment, and then she straightened and stood quite erect, her shoulder back, her chin lifted.

"I don't want to talk about it Layne," she said with a measure of hard-won composure that he found very touching. "And I'm going up to my room now. I can't take any more."

He caught her hand as she would have brushed past him and held her prisoner for a moment, standing beside her, looking down at her, his intensely blue eyes deep and warm with compassionate tenderness.

"Darling," he pleaded, "you've got to listen. You can't keep running away. I came down here for a very real purpose, Brooke: to tell you exactly where you stand in this ugly business."

"On the outside, where David and Julie put me," she said huskily.

"I wish with all my heart that was true, honey," Layne told her heavily. "But the truth is, you're right in the middle. David made a will the week before he died."

Brooke's chin was quivering a little.

"In which he left everything of which he possessed to his good friend Julie Marsh. I know that," she told him huskily. "I asked you to give her the estate — his estate."

"It's not quite that simple, Brooke. She wants his share of your estate, too," Layne gave her the ugly blow with merciful brutality.

Brooke stared at him, her eyes enormous in her white face.

"That's crazy."

Layne shook his head.

"Unfortunately, it isn't, darling," he told her reluctantly. "When the will was made, he had a hundred thousand dollars or so of his own; when he died, he was your husband and so entitled, according to law, to a share of your wealth. So Julie, seeing a chance to cut herself a very large slice of the Calloway estate, is not satisfied with having merely what David himself meant her to have."

Brooke sat down heavily, rocking from the blow.

"He could do that to me," she whispered bleakly.

"He didn't mean it that way, of course, honey," Layne assured her swiftly. "Naturally, he had no way of knowing that he was going to be dead a few hours after his marriage to you. I don't know what possessed him to make such a will."

Brooke looked up at him, and all the bitterness and the shame under which she had labored for so many months was reflected in her eyes.

"Don't you?" Her mouth was a thin, bitter line. "Julie talked him into it, of course. He was mad about Julie, and knew she'd always been hard up and had had a difficult time keeping on the fringes of the world in which she wanted so much to live." She shrugged faintly as her voice stuck in her throat.

"He came to me about the will, and I refused to have anything to do with it, of course," Layne said gently. "So he drew it up himself, with Julie's help. It's a holographic will, which means it's in his own handwriting, duly witnessed — "

"I know what a holographic will is," she told him curtly, and looked up at him. "It's legal? Acceptable in courts of law?"

Layne nodded miserably. "I've managed so far to keep Julie from filing it for probate, but it hasn't been easy," he explained. "I've warned her that if she does it without first giving you a chance to settle out of court, we'll fight it. But even though I'm convinced he was drunk as an owl when he made it, that would be impossible to prove."

"So I'll have to let her dip her greedy little paws into my entire estate and help herself to whatever she wants. Is that what you're trying to tell me?" she asked at last.

"We'll have to do our best to keep her demands within reason, of course — "

Brooke's laugh was a hollow travesty of mirth.

"Keep Julie within reason? Oh, Layne, you dreamer you!" she mocked.

Layne nodded and heaved a deep sigh, running his fingers through his close-cropped hair, his eyes deeply troubled.

"At least, Brooke, you have to see her," he began.

"I will not!"

"But, Brooke — "

She was on her feet again, and this time she evaded him and ran out of the room and away from him. From upstairs he heard the sound of a door closing hard.

10

WHEN Brooke came down to breakfast the next morning, she was pale and there were shadows of sleeplessness beneath her eyes. But she looked composed and as lovely as ever in her well-cut slacks and a thin shirt, with a sweater tossed over her shoulders.

She pushed open the swinging door into the kitchen, and Miss Bessie turned, smiled at her and said, "Breakfast is served in the dining room, Miss Brooke. Mr. Meredith is already in there."

"Mr. Meredith can come into the kitchen and have his breakfast with us," Brooke objected.

"You can go in the dining room and have breakfast with him, ma'am," said Miss Bessie firmly.

"He's no better than we are! If we

can eat in the kitchen — ”

"He's a house guest," Miss Bessie insisted firmly. "You're family. And it's up to you to entertain him, so you trot yourself into that dining room like a lady that's official hostess at Peacock Hill!"

Brooke stared at her, affronted.

Miss Bessie put her hands on her hips and looked back at Brooke, unrelenting, and it was Brooke who gave in first.

"I told him last night you were a martinet," she said.

"Soon as I get time, I'll look that word up in the dictionary, and if it's what I think it is, you'll hear from me," Miss Bessie threatened darkly. She put her hands on Brooke's shoulders and gently but firmly propelled her toward the dining room. "Trot along now; I'll bring you breakfast in a minute."

"Yessum," said Brooke meekly, and walked into the dining room, where Layne sprang up at sight of her.

"Hello," he greeted her warmly, and held her chair. "Did you sleep?"

"Of course not; did you expect me to?" Brooke answered, and shook out her napkin. "Did you? Sleep, I mean."

Layne smiled at Miss Bessie, who had followed Brooke into the room with a tall silver pot of coffee, and answered Brooke, for Miss Bessie's benefit, "Oh, yes, fine. Wonderful bed. No wonder you like it so much down here."

Brooke managed a smile to Miss Bessie, who eyed her sharply, taking in the evidences of Brooke's sleeplessness.

"Oh, I love it down here," Brooke answered gaily.

Miss Bessie went out, and Layne buttered a bit of toast, his eyes on Brooke.

"I played chess with your uncle for a while, and he has asked me to stay for the weekend. Is that all right with you?" he asked quietly.

"Well of course," Brooke answered brightly, and shook her head as he offered the toast rack. "Just juice and coffee, thanks. There's some sort of

145

dance down at Harmony Grove tonight. I'm invited, and I'm sure they would be delighted if I brought my own date along. You might enjoy it."

"If you're going to be there — " he began. And then he dropped the pretense of brittle gaiety and said roughly, "Now see here, Brooke, let's get down to cases. What have you decided?"

"About Julie? I'm going to fight her, of course," said Brooke as though there could not possibly be any other decision.

Layne nodded slowly.

"You mean you're going to contest the will," he stated rather than asked. "I was afraid you were."

"Afraid?"

"It could develop into quite an unpleasant brawl, you know," Layne warned her.

"That's what I'm counting on," Brooke told him coolly. "That's what I hope for."

"What you hope for? It won't be any

pleasanter for you than for her," Layne repeated his warning.

"Do you really think anything could be more unpleasant than what I've already been through?"

Layne's brows were drawn together and he was deep in thought.

"Of course we might be able to get it heard in chambers, instead of in open court, with the newspapers excluded."

"No!" said Brooke so sharply that he stared at her. "In open court, with as many newspapermen around as possible, and a relentless cross-examination for Julie — and for me, too!"

"Oh, look, now, honey, you don't realize what you're letting yourself in for," Layne protested.

"Oh, yes, I do," Brooke insisted grimly. "I'm letting myself in for a spot of unpleasantness that will be inconsequential after what I've already had. And I'm letting Julie in for a scandal she'll never be able to live down. And that's what I want!"

Layne frowned for a moment, and then he yielded.

"If that's how you want it — "

"It's how I want it," Brooke told him levelly, "even if it does make me out as the corniest of all living creatures, 'the woman scorned' — "

"Of course she will probably agree to settle out of court if we give her David's estate — " Layne suggested.

"There will be no settlement out of court, and she will not lay a finger on David's estate, if I win — and I'm pretty sure I will! In that case the estate will got to charity."

One look at her taut, white face told Layne it would be futile to argue with her.

"Well, at least you have come to a decision," he said dryly.

"Even if it is one you don't approve?" she mocked.

"I haven't said I don't approve."

"You don't have to. I know you so well I have only to look at you, hear the sound of your voice and know whether you agree or not," she told him frankly. "I suppose I should be big and noble and forgiving and hand her over anything she wants from me. But she took something that I wanted very much — " Her voice trailed off and her eyed widened beneath the shock of a sudden thought. "Or *did* I really want David?"

For a moment there was a startled, hopeful gleam in Layne's eyes.

"That's something only you can know, honey," he said quietly.

Brooke was still staring into space, her brows furrowed in thought.

"I suppose I must have, or I wouldn't have suffered so much when I learned the truth from him, would I?" she mused aloud.

"It was more than just your pride being hurt?" asked Layne, scarcely daring to hope the answer would be in the affirmative.

Brooke nodded slowly. "Oh, yes, I think so. I had been so much in love with him — we were going to have such a wonderful marriage." She gave a little sardonic chuckle. "It lasted for one whole hour, that wonderful marriage. But I should have known marriage was like that — not quite that brief but just a matter of a few months. Goodness knows I'd seen enough of those brief encounters called marriage in my own family and among my friends. I suppose I was lucky it didn't last any longer." Her voice quivered and was still.

Layne stood up quickly.

"If you've finished your breakfast, let's get out of here," he said roughly. "A good brisk walk is what the doctor ordered for you, my girl. Blow the cobwebs away!"

Brooke rose without argument and walked with him out of the house.

Though the morning air had a bite to it, the sun was up and spilling over the mountainside, lifting the mist from the valleys.

"Hi, this is wonderful!" said Layne,

and breathed deeply. "What's that funny smell?"

Brooke laughed. "Fresh mountain air, you city slicker," she mocked him. "Rather knocks you over after all that city smog, doesn't it? Where shall we walk? I'm a stranger here myself, and I don't know much about finding paths. From here it looks as if we walked very far we might plunge over a cliff. So how about following the road down there?"

"A thoroughly wise suggestion, my girl. I admit I have no fondness for getting lost in the wilderness — not even with you, much as I love you."

Brooke winced and cried out, "No, Layne — don't!"

"Sorry. I didn't mean to upset you," Layne told her, his jaw set and hard. "But just kick the idea around a bit in that lovely noggin of yours now and then, will you? Meanwhile, shall we walk?"

"Let's," Brooke agreed. As they walked down the drive to the road, she had a sudden inspiration. "Let's walk over and see Robin and Kirke and tell them we'll go to the dance with them tonight, shall we? Would you like to? It might be fun."

"Then by all means, let's!" Layne agreed, smiling down at her.

They set off down the road, and Brooke enlivened their walk by telling him how she had happened to meet Robin and Kirke. As Layne listened to her account, he felt a cold chill creep over him, remembering last night when he had driven up this mountain, and trying to visualize it as it had been on a night of a wild spring storm. But Brooke, who had never known such an experience before, now seemed to look on it merely as an interesting, amusing adventure.

They came at last to the long, low, sturdy log house set back from the road. Beyond it, there was the shimmer of a stream, dancing in the sunlight.

There was a gay and cheerful hail from the house and Robin, in the inevitable blue jeans and shirt, moccasins on her stockingless feet, came racing out to meet them. She slowed self-consciously as she saw Layne, but greeted them with such warmth that made Layne grateful for the fact that Brooke had found such a friend.

Brooke presented him, and Robin thrust out a hard, work-roughened hand.

"Hello," she greeted him. "I'm glad somebody's come to visit Brooke so she won't get homesick and run off back to New York."

"There's not much danger of that," said Brooke dryly.

"No, I'm afraid there isn't," Layne agreed. Robin caught by his tone, looked swiftly from him to Brooke.

"Where's your car?" she changed the subject. "Did you leave it on the road?"

"We walked over," said Brooke.

Robin's eyebrows went up in shock. "Walked?" she protested. "Why, it

153

must be at least two miles."

Brooke laughed and jerked a thumb over her shoulder in Layne's direction.

"Himself here boasts that he walked twice around the reservoir every morning before breakfast," she said.

Robin looked up at Layne, puzzled. "Is that far?" she asked.

"About six miles, give or take a bit here and there," Layne agreed.

"Before breakfast?" Robin marveled. "I'll bet you don't have just orange juice and coffee for breakfast."

"Oh, no," Layne laughed. "I add a couple of slices of toast and a soft-boiled egg."

Robin sighed and shook her head humorously.

"I guess I just won't ever understand city people," she confessed.

"Don't bother to try, Robin. It's wasted time. We don't deserve it," Brooke assured her. "Where's Kirke this morning?"

"Oh, he's down at the barn with Muley cow and her calf. He's so happy about that calf, you'd think there had never been another in the whole mountain," Robin told them.

"I seem to remember you consider Samanthy and her family quite delightful," Brooke reminded her. "Don't you like cows? And why Mooley cow? That sounds like something out of a child's comic book."

"Oh, not Mooley," Robin corrected her, laughing. "It's Muley — because the farmer who raised her bobbed her horns and now she hasn't any. They were going to be very long and sharp, and he was afraid of her."

Kirke came up the path from the barn, wiping his hands on a bit of grimy waste, and Brooke smiled as she saw him walking toward them — a tall, rugged young man in battered overalls, his ancient straw hat pushed back on his head. The Spirit of the Mountains, Brooke thought oddly.

He looked up, saw them, and a smile flashed over his lean dark face as he accelerated his pace.

"I didn't hear a car," he said when he had shaken hands with Layne and had turned back to Brooke. "Don't tell me you had a breakdown or ran out of gas again."

"Oh, no, we walked," Brooke answered lightly. "Layne wanted to. Robin says there's a new baby-calf. May I see it?"

"Of course," Kirke answered, pleased. "Maybe you'll help me find a name for her."

Layne smiled and shook his head. "I think I'll walk down and look at the brook down there. Is there good fishing around here?"

Robin's face glowed with delight.

"Oh, are you a fisherman?" she asked eagerly.

"When I get a chance."

"Then you must stay on until warm weather," said Robin eagerly. "It's too cold to fish now, but in another month — "

"I'm returning to New York tomorrow," Layne said and Kirke looked swiftly at Brooke.

"And I suppose you will be going, too." It was not a question, but a statement, and there was a tinge of regret in his voice.

"Uncle Ezra has invited me to stay on indefinitely," Brooke answered. "And I can't think of a more perfect place to spend a summer! So I'll be around for a while!"

"That's great!" said Kirke with such relief that Layne shot him a swift, startled glance. "Shall we go see the new calf? Sure you won't come along, you two?"

"Quite sure, thanks," drawled Robin. "I've *seen* a calf, and like I always say, when you've seen one, you've seen 'em all. I'm going to walk Mr. Meredith down to the creek and try to persuade him to come back later in the summer and help me catch Old Granddad."

Kirke and Brooke laughed and walked off together toward the barn.

Robin beamed up at Layne.

"You didn't really want to see the

calf, did you, Mr. Meredith?" she asked.

"I'd much rather see the creek, and the name is Layne, Robin," he assured her firmly. As they walked down the steep path to the silver shimmer of water, he added curiously, "And who is this Old Granddad you want me to help you catch?"

"Oh, the biggest catfish you ever dreamed of. I bet he'd weigh — well, golly, I've caught 'em weighing seven pounds or more, and they're babies beside Old Granddad!" she said cheerfully. "Old Granddad is a sort of legend around here; people are always claiming they've seen him and almost caught him. Kirke made me promise I wouldn't try, alone; he said Old Granddad is big enough to pull me into the pool where he lives."

"He must be a monster-fish!" Layne's eyes were shining with a born fisherman's eagerness.

"I've never seen him myself," Robin confessed. "Kirke says if I ever see a head like a bulldog's rising up out of the water, and long, droopy whiskers like a Chinaman, I should run like the dickens. I think I would, too."

"I can't say I'd blame you." Layne laughed.

"Kirke says he thinks it's really an alligator, not a catfish at all," Robin said. "But alligators don't have whiskers, do they?"

"I'm quite sure they don't, and besides, what would an alligator be doing way up here? They're tropical creatures and couldn't live in cold water."

"Oh, Kirke was only having fun; he didn't really mean it," Robin dismissed the thought carelessly, and squinted up at the sun. "I'd better be getting back to the house if we're going to have any dinner. You and Brooke will stay for dinner, won't you? And then Kirke will drive you back to the Hill in the jeep."

"Dinner?" Layne repeated, and instantly corrected himself, "of course. We'd love to."

Robin twinkled at him. "Us mountain folks has our dinner in the middle of the day, mister, not like quality folks up at Peacock Hill."

"Stop that, Robin," Layne said swiftly.

"Stop what, mister?" she asked innocently.

"Trying to sound like a hillbilly."

"Like I told Brooke the other day, that's a dirty word in these parts, mister." She kept the drawl in her voice deliberately. "We're mountain folk; we're not hillbillies."

"I mean no offense, Robin."

"Of course you didn't, Layne, any more than Brooke did, and I was only kidding." Robin laughed and tucked her hand through his arm as they went back up the steep path toward the house. "And I do hope you'll come back in the summer and go fishing. I'll show you all my favorite spots, that I've never showed anybody before. That is, if you aren't afraid of snakes."

"Well, let's just say that they are

not my favorite people." Layne grinned down at her and drew her arm closer to his side, feeling the warmth of her hand as it clung to his arm. "But I've always heard that rattlesnakes are gentlemen and always warn before they strike — "

"Which," Robin assured him flatly, "is a big fat lie! Copperheads are what we have most of in these parts, and if you watch where you're going, you're pretty safe. I've been fishing up here since I was knee-high to a tadpole, and I've never been bitten yet!"

Layne stooped down, picked up a chip of wood and held it out to her solemnly.

"Knock it," he ordered her. "Never make a boast like that without knocking wood, my girl."

Robin smothered a giggle, and as solemnly as he had offered the bit of wood rapped her knuckles on it. Layne threw the wood away and said, "Let that be a lesson to you, my poppet!"

"What's a poppet?"

"Oh, it's just a — well, I suppose a

term of endearment." Layne saw the laughter brimming in her eyes, and they went up to the house in a gale of mirth.

Brooke and Kirke, waiting for them, eyed them curiously.

"What's the joke?" asked Kirke.

"If it's that funny, share it," suggested Brooke.

Layne and Robin exchanged a merry glance.

"Shall we tell them?" asked Robin.

"Let's not," said Layne. "They wouldn't understand."

Kirke grinned at their laughing faces.

"Layne and Brooke are staying for dinner, Robin," he announced.

"Oh, no, Kirke, they're staying for *lunch*," Robin corrected him. "Dinner they have at Peacock Hill — it's an old established custom."

Kirke eyed her severely.

"You, my girl, are being fresh and auditioning for a spanking," he warned her. "And I have seldom seen a fresh kid more appropriately dressed for just

162

that. Scat into the kitchen, woman, and get the vittles on the table."

Robin wrinkled her nose at him and said loftily to Layne, "Pay him no mind; he don't mean for true more'n half of what he says."

She slid past Kirke, laughing as he raised his hand ominously, and Brooke followed her.

"Can't we help?" asked Layne.

"Goodness no! You want to get blacklisted by every upstanding mountain husband in the whole country?" protested Robin. "Men folks, they claim, have no business in the kitchen. That's women folks' work. You and Kirke settle the affairs of the nation while Brooke and I see to frying the salt pork and scrambling the eggs."

"If that's supposed to alarm me," Layne assured her, "it doesn't at all. Bacon and eggs are my favorite food."

"To be quite honest with you, any food is my favorite food at the moment," Brooke called back. "I'm famished."

163

11

MISS BESSIE came up to Brooke's room a few minutes after dinner had been cleared away and eyed with lively appreciation the frock of jade-green taffeta that Brooke had worn for dinner.

"Lije says you and Mr. Meredith are going down to the square dance in Harmony Grove, Miss Brooke," she explained her presence. "I thought maybe I could help you dress."

Brooke looked at her, puzzled.

"But, Miss Bessie, I *am* dressed," she answered.

"I was afraid of that," admitted Miss Bessie. "Afraid you'd think that was the right kind of a dress to wear to a square dance."

"Well, isn't it?"

Miss Bessie was matter of factly examining the contents of the closet and spoke over her shoulder.

"Not unless you want to stop the dance dead in its tracks, it ain't," she answered.

"Miss Bessie, are you insinuating that it's an indecent dress?" Brooke asked with some heat.

"Land o'Goshen, no! That's as silly a thing as I ever heard tell of," snorted Miss Bessie. "I don't think you'd know how to wear an indecent dress. It's just that folks in Harmony Grove have never seen a dress as pretty as that, or anybody that looks as beautiful as you do in it. You'd just about scare the men to death, and the women would hate you to pieces, and everybody'd sit around on their hands and there wouldn't be any dancing done. Here, this will have to do."

She held up a printed silk frock with a full skirt, a scooped neckline and sleeves that came to the elbow.

"You can kick up your heels in this one, which you couldn't ever do in that one that fits you like paper on the wall," Miss Bessie told her firmly. "Here, let me help you. Lije is showing Mr. Meredith what he ought to wear."

Brooke allowed herself to be helped out of the jade-green sheath and into the blue printed silk.

"I've never been to a square dance, Miss Bessie," she admitted humbly. "I'll probably fall flat on my face."

"Oh, no, you won't. Just listen to the caller and do what your partner does, and you'll be all right," Miss Bessie comforted her.

When she went into the big drawing room where Ezra and Tom were already settled at their chess game, Ezra looked up at her and smiled.

"Why, where's the pretty green dress? You looked like a — a — what's the word, Tom?"

"A dryad?" suggested Tom, smiling.

"Miss Bessie felt it wasn't suitable for a square dance," Brooke confessed.

"Oh, really? Well, probably she's right," Ezra agreed. "And you look very pretty in that — a very pretty dress."

"Thank you, darling," said Brooke, kissed his cheek, walked a few steps to Tom and kissed him, too. "Good night, both of you. We won't be late — that is, no later than we can help. We haven't the faintest notion what we're letting ourselves in for, but Miss Bessie says it will be fun."

Layne appeared in the doorway in the suit he had worn when he arrived, and he and Brooke said good night and went out into the crisp darkness.

"There's just one thing about this affair that I thoroughly dread," Layne confessed as he slid beneath the wheel of her car.

"There are a few things I dread, too, such as falling flat on my face," Brooke confessed. "What's your fear?"

"That brute of a road!" Layne admitted. "Driving up it in the darkness was bad enough; but driving down — "

"You are so right," Brooke admitted, shivering. "Robin and I went down so I could telephone you, but that was in the daytime. Don't dread it, though. Kirke will drive, if you want him to."

"Believe me, I want him to," said Layne in profound relief. "One thing I never liked about mountains — anywhere you want to go is either straight up or straight down!"

"But it's such beautiful country — once you get accustomed to it," Brooke reminded him.

"I suppose so," he answered. "Have you become accustomed to it, in the very short time you've been here?"

"Not quite," she had to admit. "But I'm hoping to before I leave."

"And that will be — ?"

"When Uncle Ezra gets tired of having me around and turns me out into a driving snowstorm — and then I'll probably seek shelter again with Kirke and Robin," she told him. "I believe I could find — maybe not happiness, but at least a measure of peace up here, Layne. It's as if I'd

168

closed the door on the past — the ugly past — and barred it."

"But if you contest David's will — "

"Don't try to talk me out of that, Layne. My mind is very firmly made up," she warned him. And there was an edge to her voice that made him glad they had by now reached the Bryant place, where Robin and Kirke came out to greet them.

Kirke readily agreed to drive, and Brooke stayed where she was in the front seat beside him. Layne helped Robin into the back seat and got in beside her.

"Be sure to tell him ghost stories to keep his mind off the road, Robin," Brooke called back to them.

"Oh, Kirke's driving, so we don't have to worry about the road tonight." Robin laughed comfortably.

"Your little sister evidently thinks very well of you," Layne suggested.

"It takes a lot of living up to, believe me," Kirke admitted over his shoulder as he started the big car and headed it down the steep, winding road.

All was quiet in Harmony Grove except for the big square Community House, obviously the scene of the dance. Here there were lights and a crowd, and laughter and the sound of 'country fiddles' sawing merrily away.

Kirke and Robin were greeted warmly, and Layne and Brooke, when they were introduced, were given a cordial welcome. Inside the big Community House, a dance was in progress when they entered, and all four stood for a moment, watching. Layne and Brooke were wide-eyed as the dancers whirled, promenaded, broke and came back together again, to the strident calls of a tall, spare old man in khaki trousers and a sweater, who stood on the platform in front of a group of musicians unlike anything the visitors had ever seen. The two fiddlers stood up, one on either side of the platform; behind them two or three men held old-fashioned brown jugs, into which they blew lustily, evoking a weird but foot-tingling rhythm. Another man was at the drums, and one held between his knees a tin tub in which a metal-covered washboard rested. The man wore thimbles on all fingers, and as he brought his hands up and down on the washboard, his own peculiar beat was added to the madness of the rest of the 'orchestra.'

Brooke looked up at Layne, who raised his eyebrows slightly and murmured, "Fantastic, isn't it?"

"But it *does* have a certain amount of rhythm," Brooke objected.

"For want of a better word," Layne murmured.

The dance broke up in a wild cacophony of more or less musical noise; and flushed, perspiring despite the chill of the night, the dancers scattered about the room.

Robin and Kirke stood in a circle of friends, to which they drew Brooke and Layne; and when the 'caller' on the platform ordered a brisk roll of drums and called out, "Choose your partners, ladies and gents, for the next set," Kirke looked at Brooke.

"Want to try it?" he asked, a twinkle in his eyes.

"Goodness, Kirke, I wouldn't know the first step."

"Sure you will," Kirke answered. "Just follow along with me, and with the people on either side of you when we join hands and promenade."

"I've never seen such intricate footwork," Brooke told him as the set began to form, with Robin, laughing, dragging Layne into it.

"We step lively," Kirke said.

The music began, and the dancers followed the tall, spare old man who sang out his orders with a lustiness, an authority that cracked like a whip. Brooke found, stumbling now and then in the intricate measures of the most complicated dance she had ever known, that her fellow dancers were pleasant, helpful, amused but not ridiculing her.

One old man, swinging her lustily, chuckled as she missed a beat.

"Takes a while to get the hang o' it, ma'am," he consoled her when she tried to apologize.

"I should think it would take a lifetime," Brooke replied, as she went once more into Kirke's arms for a swing around the floor.

"Having fun?" asked Kirke, as he whirled her about.

"I really don't know," she gasped. "I haven't had this much exercise in longer than I can remember."

Kirke danced her to a corner, out of the reach of hands that were held out to swing her into a new pattern of the dance.

"Want to stop?" he asked.

"I'm afraid I'll have to. I haven't any breath left," she panted at the back of the room.

"I'll get you a drink," he told her and threaded his way across the room, to where a make-shift counter had been set up, with huge tubs of ice holding frosty bottles of various soft drinks.

Brooke watched the dancing, wide-eyed and enthralled. There were youngsters she felt were much too young to be out of bed this late, and old men and women. She was awed to see how swiftly the children's feet moved, how unquestioningly and how correctly they followed the calls that to her were so much gibberish.

All were flushed and laughing and obviously having a wonderful time. She saw Layne and Robin; Robin was laughing up at Layne, flushed, radiant, guiding him in the various steps and patterns being called.

Brooke watched Layne's absorbed intent face and felt a small pang in her heart. Why, she asked herself passionately, could she not have loved Layne, instead of David? Was it because Layne had always seemed almost like an older brother? Was it because she had grown up so accustomed to him during their years of growing up that she could never see him in the light of someone to fall in love with?

Kirke was back, offering her a tall, frosty bottle in which he had managed to insert a straw.

"I tried to get a paper cup or a glass for you to drink out of," he apologized for the straw. "But the church circle ladies who are selling the soft drinks were outraged at the thought. Claimed everybody should drink out of a bottle, and that way there'd be no dishes to wash afterwards. I did manage to find a straw, though — all sealed up in paper, so you needn't be afraid to use it."

Brooke laughed at him. "You needn't have gone to so much bother," she protested.

Kirke sat down beside her and looked at her.

"It was no bother," he told her quietly. "I wish it had been. I'd have been delighted to go to a lot of bother for you, Brooke."

For a moment she could only

stare at him, caught by something so unexpected in his eyes that it shook her badly. Then, as though he had been as surprised as she, he looked swiftly away and made some casual comment about the dancing. And she was able to convince herself that he had meant absolutely nothing by his quiet words or by that look in his eyes.

She had been a silly fool, she told herself crossly, as the set ended and Robin and Layne came to join them, each carrying one of the cold, well-frosted bottles.

"Shall we try this next struggle, Brooke?" Layne asked when the music began once more.

"Thanks, no," Brooke answered. "I'm too old for this sort of thing — at least until I learn more about it. You and Robin go ahead; you too, Kirke, if you like. I'll learn faster by just watching."

"Sure you don't mind?" asked Kirke, when Robin and Layne had joined the set that was forming.

"Quite sure, Kirke." Brooke smiled at him. "Go find Miss Elvie. I'm sure she's dying to dance with you."

Kirke grinned at her and walked away.

Brooke watched his tall, well-knit body swing away with that effortless ease that bespeaks perfect coordination, perfect physical fitness, and remembered uneasily the small, startled moment when he had said he would like to take a lot of bother for her.

And then she saw him dancing with Miss Elvie, who looked flushed and young and happy as they moved into the forming set.

A voice spoke beside her as a very old woman settled in the next chair, and reached out a wrinkled brown hand to touch the silk of Brooke's dress.

"My, my, that's a pretty dress." Her thin old voice held a childlike admiration. "I always did like a flowery dress."

Brooke turned to her, relieved at no longer being alone with her thoughts that were taking such an alarming direction, and she and the old woman plunged into conversation.

12

IT was a little after midnight when Layne and Brooke returned to Peacock Hill, but there was still a light in the big drawing room.

"I wonder if Uncle Ezra is still up," Brooke said as they went into the house.

Ezra and Tom sat with the chessboard between them, and for a moment they were not aware of Brooke and Layne in the doorway. Ezra looked up at last, laughing as he checkmated a move of Tom's, and said, "Oh, you're back, my dear. Did you enjoy the dance?"

"As Robin would say, 'It was the most'," Brooke replied. "Uncle Ezra, you didn't wait up for us?"

Ezra seemed astonished.

"Why, of course not. What an idea! Tom and I are night owls. We rarely go to bed before two A.M. At our age, we

179

don't need much sleep," he answered as though puzzled at such a question.

"I was afraid maybe you might have waited up." Brooke felt like a fool, and her voice stumbled a bit.

"Well, you needn't have been, my dear. Tom and I are very independent old men, and Peacock Hill is 'Liberty Hall,' where we all come and go as suits our wishes," Ezra told her.

"Then I'll say good night and run along to bed," said Brooke, and kissed his cheek. She crossed to Tom and kissed him, too. "Good night, darlings — both of you."

She smiled at Layne, brushed his cheek with the tips of her fingers and left the room. The three men watched her go, and then Ezra said quietly, "If you aren't sleepy, Layne, won't you sit down? You'll be leaving tomorrow, I believe? Sure you can't stay longer? We'd be happy to have you stay."

"That's very hospitable and very kind of you, sir, but I have to get back to my office," Layne answered.

180

Ezra had obviously lost interest in the chess game, and Tom waited and watched him as he sought for words that came awkwardly.

"I think your being here has helped Brooke," said Ezra at last, and met Layne's eyes. "I'm worried about her, Layne."

"So am I, Mr. Calloway."

Ezra nodded slowly.

"You knew this man who was her husband?"

"Quite well, sir. We were college friends. In fact, I introduced them — though now I wish to heaven I hadn't." He broke off, scowling.

"Do you now?" asked Ezra. "She seems to have been very deeply in love with him. His death was a terrible blow, coming as it did so close on the heels of their marriage."

"Yes, of course," said Layne, his tone colorless because of the effort he had to make to keep out of it anything that would betray the fact that David's death had only been one more blow on top of a more savage one he himself had delivered.

"I was very touched that Brooke should come here in her grief and trouble," said Ezra. "That she will look on this as her home, that she will stay as long as she can be satisfied here, is my fondest wish."

"She seems very contented here, far more so than anywhere else I've seen her."

"I'm happy to hear that." Ezra gave him that singularly sweet smile that illuminated his lean, pale old face so rarely. "And I hope very much that you will return later on for a long visit. The summer is really very beautiful up here, though just now I'm afraid you may find that a bit difficult to believe."

Layne, who did, hoped he made his answer convincing. "Oh, no, sir, not a bit too hard to believe. Robin Bryant has offered to take me fishing if I will come back during warm weather. I should like to very much, if Brooke is still here."

"I hope she will be, and I'll look forward to seeing you then," said Ezra pleasantly, and extended his hand. "I shan't be seeing you in the morning, so I'll say goodbye now. It's been very pleasant knowing you, Layne. I hope to get to know you much better."

"Thank you, sir; I share that wish," Layne told him, and shook hands with both old men.

When he had gone, Ezra sat for a moment staring into space, pulling at his beardless lower lip, until Tom said, "Want to play any more, Ezra?"

Ezra looked up at him and then at the chess table and turned away.

"No, Tom," he answered, and scowled. "He seems a rather decent lad, doesn't he? I hope he will come back."

Tom, with the mockery permitted a lifelong friend, chuckled.

"Aren't you a bit old for that kind of thing, Ezra?" he asked.

Ezra stared at him, pretending to be puzzled.

"For what sort of thing?" he demanded, mildly incensed.

"The bow-and-arrow thing — Cupid's business."

"Oh, hush that nonsense, Tom," Ezra snorted. "I'm not trying to make a match between them — though Brooke needs a husband to look after her and I think Layne would do a good job of it. But it's none of my business — is it?"

"Not the slightest," Tom assured him firmly.

Ezra sighed heavily.

"No, I suppose not," he agreed. "But the child needs somebody to help her."

"The child, Ezra, is a woman grown, and I'm quite sure she is entirely capable of making her own romance when she's ready for it," Tom reminded him. "Her husband has been dead less than six months. Give her time to get over her loss before you start trying to push her into another man's arms."

Ezra eyed him severely.

184

"You are a very logical man, Tom, and I value you highly," he said sternly. "Your help on the books has been priceless, I don't know what I'd do without you — but I will not stand for impertinence."

"I'm not impertinent. How could I be, at our age? I'm a year older than you are; so impertinence is out of the question," Tom reminded him. "And if what Brooke does is none of my business, which it most definitely isn't, then it's only slightly less than yours. And if you wish to lose your temper because I've reminded you of that, I'll go along to bed and let you stew alone."

"Good night, Tom," said Ezra frostily.

"Good night, Ezra," said Tom, equally coldly. And suddenly both old men grinned.

"Sorry, Tom," said Ezra.

"No reason to be, Ezra," Tom answered.

"Aren't we two old fools sitting

here, trying our darnedest to stir up an argument over the affairs of a young and lovely widow? I wonder how we could be such fools!" Ezra said.

"I think it must be a sign that spring is on the way," Tom retorted. "The sap rising in old trees — why not in old men? High time we got back to minding our own business, which, at the moment, seems to me to be getting some sleep. Tomorrow's another day, you know."

Ezra nodded and said slowly, thoughtfully, "I believe Layne is in love with her."

"So do I," Tom agreed. "But that, too, is none of our business."

Layne, making an early start for the long drive ahead of him, came quietly down the stairs, and was startled when Elijah said briskly, "Good morning, Mr. Meredith. Breakfast is waiting."

"Oh, come now, Elijah, you and Miss Bessie shouldn't have bothered with breakfast," Layne answered quickly. "I

186

could have picked up something along the road."

Elijah's leathery cheeks were creased in a grin.

"Sounds a mite unsanitary," he drawled, "and anyway, Bessie wouldn't have allowed you to leave without breakfast. It's all ready and waiting."

Miss Bessie beamed at Layne as she brought his fruit juice and coffee. "You've got a nice morning for your drive, Mr. Meredith. Sun'll soon lift that mist, and it'll be a fine day."

"Thanks, Miss Bessie, for the assurance," Layne answered. And she went back to the kitchen for the bacon and eggs and toast that she considered the only fit breakfast for a man.

Layne was half through his breakfast when Brooke came in, in slacks and a sweater, smiling a good morning.

"I'm going to miss you, Layne," she told him, accepting the coffee that Miss Bessie brought her with a grateful smile.

"Well, there's an easy way to avoid

that," Layne pointed out, when Miss Bessie had gone back to the kitchen and they were alone.

"Is there? How?"

"By driving back with me."

"Oh, no, Layne, I couldn't! I don't think I can ever go back."

"You like it here so much?"

"For the present. Oh, I suppose I'll get bored and tired of it and wander on somewhere else."

"Now see here, Brooke, that's the most arrant nonsense — " Layne scolded her with unexpected sharpness — "condemning yourself to wander the earth. I never heard anything so ridiculous — "

"What would *you* suggest?" she mocked him wryly. "Interest myself in charity work? Take up a cause? Crusade?"

"I suggest that you stop feeling sorry for yourself," Layne said bitingly.

Anger flared in her eyes.

"How dare you accuse me of anything so loathsome?" she flashed.

"Because it's true and I think, deep down inside, you realize it, too, and are ashamed — as you darned well should be," Layne told her. "Sure you've had a bitter blow; you've lost a man you thought you loved."

Brooke's eyes were wide and startled. "How did you know that?" she demanded. "I mean that I only *thought* I loved David?"

"Chiefly because you'd only known him a few weeks, and you were dazzled by his good looks and his great charm."

Brooke nodded wryly. "You're perfectly right," she admitted. "And what I thought was love died when he told me the truth."

"Then come on back home with me," Layne pleaded.

Brooke looked about her at the big, mellow old room; at the windows through which the sun was creeping; at the scene outside, the bare trees tossing in the fresh morning breeze, the ancient pines like dark sentinels against the rocky sides of the mountain.

"Home," she repeated, as though she tasted the word and liked its savor on her tongue, "Layne, I *am* home. For the first time in my life, I feel really at home — and it's a wonderful feeling."

Layne's eyes upon her were tender with an understanding she felt quite touching.

"I'm glad, honey," he said gently. "Well, I have to get along if I'm going to be back in the office in time to take my case to court. It's my biggest one to date, and I'm excited about it."

"Oh, Layne, and I haven't even let you tell me about it," she mourned as she got up and walked with him out of the house and to his waiting car. "I've been so locked up in my own problems, I haven't even asked about yours. I'm ashamed."

Layne laughed, "You needn't be. It was you and your problems that brought me down here, which should indicate I was much more concerned with them than with my client. Anyway, it's been wonderful seeing you, honey, and I can go back now with my mind at ease about you. I've met Uncle Ezra and the Bryants and Miss Bessie and Elijah, so I'll know you are in good hands."

"You're sweet, Layne," said Brooke, and framed his face between her two hands and kissed him.

Layne caught his breath and went rigid. His arms reached for her, then dropped at his sides. His face was gray and set, his eyes bleak.

"Don't do that." His voice held a barely restrained violence. "Not unless you mean it — and I know you don't. So cut it out, will you?"

Brooke stood a foot away from him, looking up at him. There was a mist of tears in her eyes, and her smile was faint and tremulous.

"If I'd had a nickel's worth of sense, Layne darling, it would always have been you — if only you'd told me." Her voice shook slightly, and she went on, "I'm very fond of you, Layne; you're my favorite person. Isn't that, maybe, enough?"

"No," Layne cut in sharply, "not nearly enough. I love you, Brooke — but unless you love me, too — then it would be no good."

"I wish I did. Oh, Layne, I wish I did!"

He managed a smile that was little more than a grimace.

"So do I, honey. But you don't, and that's that," he said firmly, and got into his car.

"You'll come back, Layne?" she pleaded.

His eyes took her in and it was as though he had embraced her.

"Oh, yes, I'll come back," he promised.

"Soon, Layne?"

"Robin invited me for the fishing, and your uncle invited me, too — so I'll be back before too long," Layne answered, and lifted his hand in a little gesture of leave-taking, as the car rolled down the drive and out of sight.

Brooke stood where he had left her for a long, long moment, and then she moved off down the drive.

13

THE days slid into weeks, and the weeks slid by, and Brooke was scarcely conscious of their passing. She had never known it was possible just to sit relaxed and let waves of peace flow over her. She helped Miss Bessie as much as she was allowed to; she followed Elijah into the greenhouse, and helped him repot plants that would be set out of doors in the ground as soon as the ground warmed sufficiently to nourish them. She came to the dinner table in the evening, flushed and bright-eyed, and delighted the two old men with her gaiety.

She saw a great deal of Kirke and Robin, and they became firm friends.

She drove the two miles down to see them one afternoon in late May. There was no sign of life about the house, and she got out of the car and listened, oddly disappointed, until she heard the sound of hammering from the barn and walked down there to find Kirke mending a cow stall.

"Hi, mister," she called gaily. And Kirke dropped the hammer and came swiftly to greet her, his lean brown face illuminated by a delighted smiled.

"Oh, hello there." There was something in the eager warmth of his voice, something in his eyes, that absurdly enough made her feel confused, even shy.

"Where's Robin?" she asked quickly.

"Oh, she's gone down to visit Miss Dovie and take her a pie she baked for her," Kirke answered. "Did you want to see her?"

"I wanted to see both of you, of course," Brooke answered, and added, "If you're not too busy, Kirke, I've just had a wonderful idea."

"I'm never too busy to listen to wonderful ideas," Kirke answered, and guided her across the lane and to the house. "Shall we sit here on the porch? It's much too pleasant to go inside, don't you think?"

"Oh, much," Brooke agreed, and dropped down on the steps, drawing one slack-clad knee up, encircling it with her arms as she lifted her face to sniff delightfully of the soft, sun-drenched air. "In an hour or so it will be cold enough to go inside and start a fire, but right now it's perfect! Oh, I do love it so up here!"

"That's wonderful to hear," said Kirke with frank delight.

"Want to hear my wonderful idea?" she said hurriedly.

"Well, of course."

"I want to raise peacocks," she said eagerly.

Kirke stared at her, his brows drawn together in a frown.

"Raise peacocks?" he repeated as though quite sure he had not heard her correctly. "For heaven's sake, Brooke — why?"

"Well, it seems silly to me to have

a place called Peacock Hill, and not a peacock within miles," she pointed out reasonably enough. "So I thought it would be fun to buy a pair and raise some."

"You don't buy a pair of peacocks, City Gal!" Kirke mocked her, amused, intrigued. "You buy a peacock and four or five pea-hens. The hens lay four, possibly five eggs a year; and it takes a year for the babies to grow into whatever they're going to be — peacock or pea-hens. Raising peacocks, Brooke, is a long-time proposition. It's not like raising chickens, or even turkeys. Peacocks are a tricky business. Why do you want to raise them, anyway?"

Brooke made a little gesture that wasn't quite a shrug. "Oh, I just thought it might be a hobby. And they'd look so decorative, strutting across the terrace at sunset, their fans spread. I'd want white ones of course."

"It would be a nice hobby for Elijah, only I doubt he'd appreciate your saddling him with them."

197

"Oh, but I meant to take care of them myself," Brooke protested.

"But after you go away, Brooke — "

She tilted her chin a trifle.

"I am not going away," she said evenly, "at least not for a long, long time. Oh, I will have to run up to New York for a few days, perhaps early in June, but the case shouldn't last more than a couple of days."

Kirke asked, puzzled. "The case?"

Brooke drew a deep breath and said quietly, "You know about me, of course, Kirke. My husband was killed an hour or so after our wedding."

"I read about it in the newspapers."

"I thought you probably did," Brooke went on. "What you don't know is that one reason my husband was driving so crazily that he smashed up was that he and I had just had a terrific row."

"You needn't tell me, Brooke, unless you really want to." His tone was gentle.

"I'd rather you knew, Kirke," she answered, and was obscurely puzzled that this should be so. "You see, after the ceremony and the reception, while I was getting dressed to start on our honeymoon trip, David came and told me that he wasn't really in love with me after all."

Kirke made an explosive sound of anger and compassion, while Brooke went steadily on, her eyes on the scene about them.

"You see, while I'd been so busy making all the wedding arrangements because I felt it had to be really spectacular, he was busy falling out of love with me and in love with someone else."

"But why didn't he come to you and tell you so before the wedding?" Kirke demanded sharply.

Brooke's mouth was a thin, twisted line.

"I think because Julie wouldn't let him," she said dryly. "Or I may be giving him credit he doesn't deserve. Anyway, he said that we could get a 'nice, quiet divorce in Paris', and there would be no scandal. He claimed that he wouldn't break our engagement publicly, because he didn't want any scandal for me. Big of him, wasn't it?"

Kirke could think of nothing to say that would be suitable for a woman's ears.

"Anyway," she went on after a moment, "I was so dazed that I refused even to consider a divorce. We had a thumping quarrel; we screamed at each other as if we'd been married ages, instead of just hours! He finally plunged out of the house, and the next thing I knew he was dead."

Kirke looked at her, frowning.

"You think people who've been married a long time inevitably fight?" he asked, and was honestly puzzled.

"Well, don't they?" she challenged. "People I know do."

"People I know usually like each other well enough to arbitrate rather than fight," Kirke said with a rueful grin.

"I suppose divorces aren't as easy here as among the people I know," she confessed humbly. "I hate easy divorces. That was the reason I wanted a truly spectacular wedding: because I felt it was going to be for always. My mother cabled she couldn't get over for this marriage but would surely make the next one! You see? And then for David to stand there, still in his wedding clothes, and tell me — "

She dropped her face in her hands for a moment, and Kirke put his arms about her shaking shoulders, trying to comfort her as he would have tried to comfort Robin.

"Don't cry, honey, he wasn't worth it," he told her gently.

Brooke drew a deep breath, raised her head and looked at him.

"So now you see why I have to go to New York, to contest his will," she managed, and reached into her pocket for her handkerchief.

"Contest his will?" Kirke repeated, puzzled.

"He made one the day before the wedding, leaving everything he had to Julie," said Brooke huskily. "And of course I'm not going to let her have it."

Kirke stared at her, and his arm dropped. His brow was furrowed in a bewildered frown.

"But surely the money couldn't be that important to you," he protested.

"Oh, the money doesn't mean a thing. It's not more than a hundred thousand dollars, perhaps less," she said carelessly. "That was one of his reasons for wanting to marry me, and move into the Calloway estate and so-called social position. He hadn't any, really; and I'd been born to the circles he felt were rightfully his. He was pretty explicit about all that when he told me he wanted me to divorce him. And now Julie is standing waiting for me to make her a present of the money. Layne says she can, if she wants to — and knowing Julie, I'm sure she'll want to make a claim on me for David's 'share'."

Kirke was silent for so long that she finally turned her head and looked at him. She saw a man who was a stranger to her. This was a Kirke she'd never seen before, his jaw so rigid that a small muscle leaped along it, and his eyes filled with something so like contempt that her own widened with shock.

"So after running away from the publicity that followed his death, you're now going back to bring a thousand times more of it down on your head, and this time it will be an ugly scandal. Why? Surely you don't care that much for money. Or if you do, I don't know you at all, Brooke."

"I've told you — it isn't the money!" Brooke insisted. "It's just that I won't let her break up my marriage."

"It wasn't much of a marriage, you must admit."

"It was all I had, all I wanted. Oh, I know it sounds shabby and cheap to you."

"Not cheap," Kirke cut in. "Most

definitely, not cheap. But you're making yourself cheap."

Brooke's eyes flashed with fury.

"How dare you say that!"

"Because Layne is so crazy about you that he'd never dare, and it's way past time that somebody should say it." Kirke's tone was biting. "Just to 'get even' with this Julie, purely out of spite and malice, you're going into court and fight over what must seem to both of you a handful of copper coins."

"Not to Julie it isn't!" Brooke insisted harshly. "Julie's always been broke, and hanging on the outer fringes of the world she feels she should star in. A lot of us have wondered how she manages to dress well enough to attend such affairs as she's invited to attend. She can't play *that* good a game of bridge."

Kirke stood up, looking down at her with contempt. "I find I don't know you at all, Brooke," he said levelly. "I'm not even sure that I want to."

Brooke rose swiftly, facing him, her head erect, her eyes blazing.

"Oh, you men are all alike," she hurled at him childishly. "You and Layne think I should just hand over to her anything she wants. Well, I'm not going to do it. She's going to be punished."

"For daring to fall in love with a man the rich and social Miss Brooke Calloway wanted?"

"Oh, she wasn't in love with him."

"How can you know that?"

"Her kind doesn't fall in love — not with a man, anyway. Their eyes are on his bank account." Her spiteful voice died to silence beneath his look of utter disgust.

"And in order to punish her, you're going into court and show yourself up as spiteful, greedy, avaricious — "

"I am not!" she blazed. "I'll give David's money to charity."

"Anything to keep it from going where he wanted it to go?"

"Oh, I suppose you think I should

be big and noble and stand aside and let her have what she wants?" she flung at him savagely.

"I think you should do, as I'm sure you have always done, exactly what you want to do, regardless of the consequences," he told her, his tone so quiet after her own anger that it seemed to crackle.

"What consequences?" she asked after a moment.

"If you can't see what's sure to happen — "

"Oh, you mean the newspapers and all that? That will be for Julie to worry about. My position, as David's wife, is quite secure."

"Even when the date on the will proves it was made the day before the wedding?" Kirke pointed out with deceptive mildness, his eyes hard and cold.

Brooke breathed deeply, her hands clenched so tightly that the nails bit small half-moons in her palms.

"I will not let her have David's

estate!" she said through her teeth, and turned, running, stumbling a little as she reached her car.

She whirled it about and raced up the lane, and Robin, coming up the road in the jeep, jammed on the brakes and almost stood on her head to escape a collision.

14

MISS BESSIE and Elijah eyed Brooke curiously as the days passed, but without letting her realize it. In fact, she was so absorbed in her own unpleasant thoughts that she was scarcely aware of anything that went on around her.

"Wonder what ails her, Bessie?" Elijah asked one morning when she had snapped a negative answer to his mild suggestion she might like to help him pot some geraniums to bring in the house, and had slammed out of the house for a walk.

Clearing the table, Miss Bessie paused and looked down at her husband, just finishing his third cup of coffee.

"Men!" she sniffed disdainfully.

"Now what's that supposed to mean?" Elijah demanded wrathfully.

"Wondering what ails Miss Brooke, when any woman would know without asking. She's lonesome, that's what ails her. She misses Mr. Meredith, of course," Miss Bessie assured him as though she spoke to a child of five who wasn't very bright.

"Oh," said Elijah, with the air of one on whom a bright light had tardily dawned.

"'Oh' is right," Miss Bessie assured him. "Wouldn't surprise me none if she suddenly upped and went back to New York, unless he comes back pretty soon."

"Suppose you're right," Elijah agreed. "We'll miss her. So'll Mr. Ezra and Mr. Tom. They've been right bright every night at dinner since she's been here."

"Imagine they'll get over missing her sooner than you and me will." Miss Bessie sighed. "Been right pleasant having her here."

"Sure has," Elijah agreed.

Brooke came in from a walk late one

209

afternoon, tired and hoping she had walked hard enough and far enough to be able to sleep. As usual, since the front door was seldom unlocked, she came in through the kitchen and would have passed through and on to the stairs without a word if Miss Bessie hadn't stopped her.

"There's a lady waiting to see you, Miss Brooke."

Brooke stopped short, her eyes wide.

"A lady? What does she want?"

"To see you, Miss Brooke. Mr. Meredith brought her."

Brooke cried out eagerly, "Layne is here?"

"He was, Miss Brooke, but he's gone."

"Gone?" Brooke repeated incredulously. "Gone where?"

"Now as to that, I couldn't say, Miss Brooke," Miss Bessie answered. "He let the lady out and went tearing off. And the lady came to the front door and said she wanted to see you, so I took her into the drawing room and fixed her a pot of tea. She's still there."

Brooke brushed past and along the hall. She came to a halt in the doorway, staring with unbelieving eyes at the woman who sat at ease within a big chair beside the tea table.

For a moment she and Julie Marsh merely studied each other with cool, unfriendly eyes, and then Julie said quietly, "Hello, Brooke. You're looking well."

"What are you doing here?"

"Waiting to talk to you."

Brooke's head went up and her eyes were frosty.

"I can't think of anything in the world you and I have to talk about," she said through her teeth.

"I can," said Julie quietly. "David's will."

Brooke's mouth thinned and twisted in bitter contempt.

"That we will talk about in court," she said sharply.

"Oh, no, we won't, Brooke. That's why I've come to see you," Julie answered in that quiet, even voice that was so unlike her usual gay, vivacious tone. "We're not going into court to shame and degrade David's memory. I've come to tell you that you may have the estate without any fight. At that price, I don't want it."

Brooke blinked and drew a hard breath, her hands clenched tightly as she dropped into a chair, hating herself because her knees would no longer support her.

"At what price?" she asked at last.

"The price of an ugly scandal that will make people think of David as a graceless scoundrel, a man who married you for that miserable money you are so proud of," said Julie dryly. "Because he wasn't like that at all. He was fine and decent and honorable."

"So much so that an hour after our wedding, he asked me to divorce him?" sneered Brooke.

"So much so that he wouldn't jilt you at the church door as I asked him to do," Julie answered quietly. "We found that we were deeply in love. But you had made such elaborate plans for the wedding, and throwing you over at the last minute would have made an ugly mess. So he went through with the wedding, trusting to your decency to give him a divorce when you got to Paris."

"Which, of course, wouldn't have made 'an ugly mess'?" Brooke inserted.

Julie's lovely eyebrows went up slightly.

"Well, since when has a divorce, secured quietly and decently, made a mess in our circles, Brooke? Be realistic!"

"Realistic!" Brooke spat the word out.

Julie studied her coolly for a long moment.

"You were never really in love with him, were you?" she asked at last.

"Why else would I have been planning to marry him?"

"Oh, I imagine you were a bit tired of 'bachelor girl' apartments, even

213

the luxurious ones you were able to afford, and you wanted a good-looking, attractive man around to be host at your parties, and to look after train and plane tickets when you traveled. Who knows why a woman like you wants a man around? You're so in love with Brooke Calloway there isn't room in your emotions for anyone else."

"And of course *you* are different." Brooke's voice was shaking a little, but the weight of fury and hostility steadied it slightly.

Julie nodded, her eyes narrowed a little against the smoke of her cigarette.

"I worshipped David," she said in that level, even voice that had a faint touch of huskiness. "And he loved me very deeply. I'd have eloped with him twenty-four hours after I met him, if he had let me. But that was only a couple of weeks before the date you'd set for your wedding. We fought against being in love with each other."

"Oh, I'm sure you did!" Brooke's tone flung the words at her like sharp pebbles. "But of course it was 'bigger than both of you', wasn't it?"

Julie ignored the venom in the cliché and said quietly, "Corny as that sounds, it's quite true. When we finally realized that we had something so wonderful that we couldn't let it go, I begged David to tell you — three days before the wedding. But you'd made such a production out of the wedding, he felt it would be inhuman to throw you over then. And he was sure that you'd understand when he tried to explain to you and that you'd let him go. That's why he waited until after the ceremony. I didn't want him to; I didn't trust you, you see. Knowing you didn't really love him — "

"I don't think I care to hear any more — " Brooke began.

"Oh, but you're going to, Brooke," Julie insisted. "That night, when he told you the truth, and you rounded on him and said you were his wife and you'd never let him go — he knew then that I had been right. He telephoned me and asked me to meet him; said we'd go away together and then, from sheer pride, you'd have to let him go. He was hurrying to meet me when he crashed."

For a moment her dearly bought control gave way and she hid her convulsed face behind her hands, and Brooke could only sit and study her, shaken to the very depths of her being.

"Why did you wait so long to tell me this? Why didn't you come to see me sooner about David's will?"

Julie drew a deep, hard breath, dropped her hands and clenched them so tightly in her lap that the nails cut her flesh.

"I cracked up," she said evenly. "I've just been released from a sanatorium for the mentally disturbed."

She smiled at Brooke's shocked expression and nodded.

"Oh, yes, I was mentally disturbed. I was so shocked and heartbroken by David's death that I wanted to die, too, and when I found out that I was in a sanatorium for treatment — well, the only thing I wanted to do was stay there. It didn't make any difference where I was, since I could never be with David again."

Brooke whispered, inexpressibly shocked, "I didn't know, Julie. I never *dreamed* — "

"I'm sure you didn't," said Julie. "You were so busy playing the role of the bereaved wife that you didn't realize anyone else existed."

"I *was* bereaved."

"Sure, of a man to 'host' your parties; not of the man you loved," Julie pointed out relentlessly. "Then you found out about David's will and decided I had to suffer as you had suffered."

Suddenly her voice gained strength, the strength lent by an almost uncontrollable anger. "How dare you think you can make me suffer any more than you've already done, by driving David to his death?"

"I didn't."

"Oh, yes, you did! If you hadn't been so arrogant in your wicked, self-righteous pride, if you'd been decent and promised to free him — " Julie broke of and stood up. "Well, you can have his estate. It's been appraised at a little under a hundred thousand, invested so that it brings an income of eight to ten thousand a year, which is less than you pay your housekeeper. To me, it would mean — but never mind about that. Fighting over it in court would be a horror I won't even think about. Layne will arrange everything so it will come to you."

"Where is Layne?" asked Brooke. "I didn't see his car."

"He's gone to make arrangements for me to spend the night with some friends of his — Bryant, I think, is the name," answered Julie.

"Why, Julie, you can stay here."

"Under the same roof with you? Thanks, no!" Julie's voice shook. "Layne will drive me to Asheville in the morning, and I'll get a plane back to New York. He said he was sure the Bryants would have me, and he'd be back for me. I wish he'd come!"

"I'll drive you to the Bryants', Julie, if you insist on going. I'm sure they'll be happy to have you," Brooke said stiffly. "I hope you don't mind riding in a car with me."

Julie's eyes, that were so blue that they were like pansies, swept Brooke with a look of loathing, but she nodded.

"I don't mind, if it's not far," she said grimly.

"It's about two miles, Julie — if you'll come with me?"

Brooke was quite formal, as she led the way around to the drive where her car stood.

Julie got in, apparently on the verge of collapse.

"I'm sorry you've been so ill, Julie," Brooke said awkwardly as the car slid down the drive.

"I'm all right now," said Julie huskily. "I've learned to live with the knowledge

I'll never see David again. Now I've got to find work, something to do that will keep me busy enough not to spend twenty-four hours a day just thinking about him. He was such a wonderful person."

She glanced at Brooke, lifted her hands in a small gesture, then let them fall in her lap.

"But then you never really knew him, so you couldn't know that about him," she said drearily.

As the big car turned in at the lane leading down to the log house, Brooke said swiftly, "Julie, I don't want David's estate — I wouldn't touch it. Layne will know how to see to it that it comes to you — every penny of it."

Julie studied her for a moment in the twilight, and then she said huskily, "Thanks."

And that was all.

As the car slid to a stop, Robin came running out to the car, followed by Layne and Kirke.

"Oh, hello, Brooke," Robin greeted

her, and turned eagerly to Julie. "And you're Julie, of course. We're tickled silly that you're going to spend the night with us. Your room is all ready."

Julie murmured her thanks and, without looking back at Brooke, walked with Robin toward the house, where Kirke greeted them and they went inside. Kirke had not so much as looked at Brooke, and her heart twisted a little, even as she turned to Layne.

"You might have stayed long enough at Peacock Hill to say hello to me," she told him tautly.

"I was coming back for Julie, and I expected to see you then," Layne told her unsmilingly.

"I'm sure you'll be happy to know I no longer have the faintest intention of contesting David's will," Brooke told him.

"Good! I'm glad," said Layne, and his tone told her how much he meant it.

Robin came hurrying back. She linked her arm with Layne's and beamed at Brooke.

"We're hi-jacking your company, Brooke," she announced happily. "Layne's staying here for the night, too."

"Oh, but Layne — " Brooke began a sharp protest.

"We're leaving very early in the morning to get Julie on a plane that leaves the airport in Asheville at 5:20," Layne explained. "It was the only reservation she could get for the next couple of days, and she took it. So it will be easier for us to leave here at 3:30, which is about the time we'll have to go, than for me to sleep at Peacock Hill and come back here to pick her up."

"I'm going, too," Robin announced gaily. "Oh, only to Asheville, of course; not to New York. Layne asked me to ride over with him, so he wouldn't have to come back alone. And of course I had to be coaxed very hard — for almost five seconds.

Brooke's eyes were locked with

Layne's, and to them both Robin was like a prattling child to whom neither of them really listened.

"Oh, then you are coming back, Layne?" Brooke asked, her tongue feeling dry as dust in her mouth.

"Oh, of course," Layne answered quickly. "I'm taking a couple of weeks' vacation."

"Kirke and I know how Mr. Ezra feels about house guests, so we're shanghaiing Layne, and he's going to stay with us. That way he and I can get up at the break of dawn and go fishing," Robin boasted happily.

"I see," said Brooke, and set the motor of the big car humming. "Well, have a nice vacation, Layne. I'm sure you'll enjoy it. If you have a spare moment or two, drop in at Peacock Hill. Uncle Ezra and I will be glad to see you — Miss Bessie and Elijah, too."

She shot the car back up the drive in reverse before either of them could answer her, and Robin stared after the car for a moment before she looked up at Layne, who was scowling thoughtfully.

"Is she mad about something?" Robin asked hesitantly.

"Oh, let's say she's annoyed." Layne managed a smile.

"I guess maybe she didn't like our hi-jacking her company," said Robin wistfully.

"There's probably more to it than that," Layne answered cautiously.

15

A LITTLE later, Robin emerged from the room assigned to Julie and said worriedly, "She's worn out. I've persuaded her to go to bed and let me bring her supper on a tray. She says she doesn't want any supper, but I'm going to fix her some soup and a glass of milk."

"That will be fine, Robin," Layne answered gratefully. "She's been very ill, and the trip down here was a strain."

Kirke said quietly, "Then she shouldn't go back to New York tomorrow. Do you think we could persuade her to spend a few days or even a week here, until she is stronger?"

"Oh, Layne, could we?" Robin begged eagerly.

"I think she'd be very pleased, if

you're sure it's not an imposition — "
Layne began.

"Imposition my foot!" Robin protested happily. "You know how we love having company. And a week or two here — why, look what it did for Brooke. She was in almost as bad shape as Julie when she first came — and look at her now! She's just blooming with health."

"Yes," said Layne dryly, "just blooming with health."

"Layne, what caused Julie's illness? I mean if it was a disease, we might have to be sure we can get a doctor if she needs one — that is, if she'll stay," Robin asked.

"She has been very ill from grief and shock, not from a disease that a doctor could cure," Layne said quietly. "She was very much in love; the man she loved was killed in a car accident while he was hurrying to her. Julie cracked up from the shock. She has been in a sanatorium since September."

Kirke was staring at him, startled.

"Oh, is Julie the one?" he asked.

For a moment Layne met his eyes, startled, and then he asked quietly, "Oh, you know about that?"

Kirke nodded, his eyes on his pipe. "Brooke told me a few weeks ago."

He stood up before Layne could manage an answer, muttered something about 'chores' and went out into the cold, sweet spring night.

Puzzled by the cryptic exchange between the two men, Robin waited for Layne to explain. When he didn't, she shrugged and went out of the room to the kitchen.

Layne sat on for a long moment, staring straight before him. So Brooke had told Kirke about David and Julie. Had she also told him that she was going to contest David's will? Tonight, just a little while ago, she had told him she had changed her mind. No wonder Julie was exhausted, for it must have been quite a session the two had had . . .

Brooke slammed the car door and

walked across the back porch and into the house.

"You'll have to hurry, Miss Brooke. It's almost seven," Miss Bessie told her. "And where's Mr. Meredith. His room is ready."

"I'm not coming down to dinner, Miss Bessie, and Mr. Meredith is not visiting us, but the Bryants," Brooke said grimly, and stalked across the room and up the stairs, leaving Miss Bessie to stare after her wonderingly.

In her own room, Brooke stood for a moment. And then, her mouth a thin taut line, she hauled out her suitcases and started to pack. And then she caught her breath and put her hands over her face and dropped into a chair. What was the good of packing when she hadn't the faintest idea where to go? Also, everything within her rebelled against the thought of leaving Peacock Hill — of leaving the mountains — of leaving — She cut the thought of Kirke off sharply, and was so startled that it had even come into her mind that she sat wide-eyed and appalled.

Why should she mind leaving Kirke, for heaven's sake? He was less than nothing to her; a man from another world who could never be anything but a stranger to her. And yet, if that were true, why had it hurt so unbearably when she had seen the disgust in his eyes, heard the contempt in his voice when she had blurted out the truth about why she would be going back to New York?

She was still sitting there when Miss Bessie knocked and came in.

"You're not coming down to dinner?" Miss Bessie demanded curtly.

Angry, jerked out of her miserable thoughts by Miss Bessie's curtness, Brooke said haughtily, "I told you I wasn't."

Miss Bessie stood with her fists on her hips, her usually kindly eyes cold and hard.

"Mr. Ezra's very worried about you. And Mr. Ezra is a gentle, kind old man who was living here in peace and quiet, just the way he wanted to live and the way he deserves to keep on living, until you came barging in here and got him all upset," Miss Bessie stated in a flat, hard tone that made Brooke gasp. "Now you've got him worrying about you. And at his age, and in his frail health, that's bad for him."

Brooke stammered furiously, "Why you — "

"And don't you start none of that nonsense about: 'How dare you talk to me like that!'" Miss Bessie cut in sharply. "I'm not only Mr. Ezra's housekeeper; I'm what you might call his nurse. Lije and me have looked after him and loved him and taken care of him; and I don't propose for you to come in here, with all your lah-de-dah airs and graces, and set him worrying about you. And that's what he's doing right this minute. He's always had a fine appetite for his dinner; and now he's just picking at it, and wondering what has happened to you and if you're ill and should we have a doctor — "

Brooke said huskily, "I'm sorry, Miss Bessie. I guess I've been pretty selfish."

"I'll say 'Amen' to that," Miss Bessie assured her grimly. "Reckon maybe you've always been, but there hasn't been anybody to point it out to you until now. But I'll fight you tooth and claw if you don't get yourself down them stairs and convince Mr. Ezra there's nothing wrong with you except that you've had a fight with Mr. Meredith."

"I will, Miss Bessie." Brooke heard a voice touched with unaccustomed humility, that she scarcely recognized as her own. "I'll get dressed."

"There's no time for that," snapped Miss Bessie. "Him and Mr. Tom are halfway through dinner, neither one of them eating enough to keep a bird alive, they're that worried about you. So get on down there and convince them you're all right."

"I will, Miss Bessie, if you think seeing me in slacks won't upset them."

"Not seeing you is what's upsetting

them," snapped Miss Bessie, and paused at the door to say off-handedly, with a slight softening of her tone, "Sorry I had to be rough with you, but seemed like somebody had to tell you the time o' day, in a manner o' speaking."

"You're quite right, Miss Bessie, and thank you," said Brooke in that same unaccustomed tone of humility.

As they walked downstairs side by side, Miss Bessie said comfortingly, "Now don't you worry none about Mr. Meredith staying with the Bryants. It's just because he thinks Mr. Ezra is upset by company; and Robin must seem like a child to a man like Mr. Meredith."

Brooke stared at her, but Miss Bessie gave her a friendly pat and went on to the kitchen.

Brooke went into the dining room, where both old men greeted her with such pleasure that she felt a stab of shame that she had been so selfish as not to realize her duty as a guest, if nothing else.

She kissed them both, took her place and said gaily, "I *do* apologize for coming to dinner in slacks. I went for a long walk and got lost, and when I got back there wasn't time to dress, and I thought I'd eat in my own room."

"Now you mustn't ever do that, my dear," Ezra assured her, smiling. "You look lovely in whatever you wear. Tom and I enjoy seeing you at the table with us, and afterwards in the drawing room. I daresay it must be very dull for you here with two old codgers like us, but it makes us very happy to have you here."

"Thank you, darling," said Brooke, and smiled at Elijah as he put food before her.

"Will Layne be coming back soon? I know you must miss him," said Ezra innocently.

"Oh, Layne is here," said Brooke lightly. "He's staying with Robin and Kirke Bryant."

Ezra put down his fork, and his bushy white brows drew together.

"But why isn't he staying here? I invited him to stay here when he came back, didn't I, Tom? I meant to," he protested.

"Oh, he brought a friend down with him, and I suppose he felt it would be an imposition to invade Peacock Hill with an extra guest," Brooke explained.

"But I'm sure we have a great many more guest rooms at Peacock Hill than the Bryants have," Ezra objected, puzzled.

"Let's not worry about it, darling," said Brooke with determined lightness. "He knows he's welcome here, and perhaps when his friend is gone we'll see something of him."

"Well, I hope so — for your sake, my dear!"

"For *my* sake?" Brooke laughed.

"Well, it's only natural that someone young and beautiful should get bored living in a place like this surrounded by old people," Ezra pointed out.

"I could never be bored here, darling," Brooke told him, her voice shaken with sincerity. "I love it here. It's the only home I've ever known!"

"That's good to hear, my dear," said Ezra. And Brooke saw that he was eating his dinner with his usual healthy appetite.

She looked from one gentle, kind old man to the other. They were living here in an age that she felt had long since vanished, never to return; they seemed completely insulated against the modern world of stress and strain and tension; she wondered if they knew what the world outside was like.

"How's the book coming along?" she asked Ezra, smiling.

Puzzled, he asked, "The book?"

Brooke looked from one to another. "Aren't you working on a book of Old World history?" she asked.

Ezra laughed gently. "A book, my dear? We're now on Volume Six, and there are still eight filing cases of notes and memos and research material we have gathered over the years and that we must put into proper form while we still have some time left to us."

"I feel terribly ignorant, but who is your publisher? I don't suppose anybody as stupid as I am would know even the titles," Brooke apologized.

"Oh, the books aren't to be published, Brooke dear," Ezra protested, slightly scandalized at the thought.

"Because we like keeping busy, and the period in history fascinates us, and when you grow old, you have to find something that interests you and that you want to work very hard on, or you'll wither on the vine and blow away, leaving nothing behind to let the world know you ever existed," Ezra explained as though she should have realized that without even asking.

"But so much work, Uncle Ezra — why not have them printed privately, yourself? Why, colleges and high schools might be very interested."

Ezra looked across the table at Tom, his brows going up.

"What do you think, Tom?" he asked.

"Well, it's something to think about," Tom agreed cautiously, and smiled at Brooke. "See how much we need you here? It would never have occurred to either of us to have the books published. We were working on them for our own pleasure."

"If they please you, then the chances are very good they'd please a lot of people — students, historians, college boys and girls. Why, I bet you could find a publisher easily," Brooke insisted rashly, and had a momentary qualm. Was she encouraging them to do something that would end in bitter disappointment for them? How could she know if such books could find a publisher willing to take a chance on accepting something that might have a strictly limited appeal? But at least she had given them something to think about; and having the books published privately should not be too expensive. It would be something that would give point and scope to what they were doing, whatever became of the idea.

16

THE sun was not yet up when Layne and Robin slipped through the dew-drenched trees and brush down to the big flat rock above the deep pool that was her favorite fishing spot. Here was where Old Grandad was seen most often, and she had never given up hope that she might catch him.

The morning air was crisp and sweet with a thousand scents that Layne could not identify but that he enjoyed nonetheless. He looked down at Robin as she forced her way through the brush, laughing over her shoulder at him as she insisted that she had a path through here, though admitting that it had grown up a bit since last fall.

"Grown up a bit, indeed," Layne derided as he dodged a low-growing branch and tripped over an exposed root. "You need a machete to chop your way through this."

Robin laughed. "Well, if there was a nice wide path, other fishermen would be able to get here too easily and there wouldn't be any fish left for us."

"You've got a point there," Layne agreed, and swore under his breath as a blackberry branch slashed at his face.

They came out at last on a tiny clearing, where a huge flat rock thrust out above the brawling stream. The pool here was very deep, between the rocks; beyond the pool toward the other side, embroidered with mountain laurel, the river rushed on in a white foam.

"We have to be very quiet," Robin whispered cautiously, and Layne looked at her young, radiant face and felt a deep tenderness for her youthful happiness.

"I mean they'll go and hide if they hear us," she told him softly, baiting her hook. She flung it expertly to the center of the pool where the cork bobbed gently. "Want me to bait your hook?" she whispered to Layne.

"I do not. The idea! I'm insulted. Who do you think I am, a city slicker? I've fished before," he assured her, his voice pitched to a tone of outrage that made her go "sh-h-h-h!"

They fished in companionable silence for a while. Whether they caught anything or not, whether they so much as got a bite, didn't matter a bit to either of them. Just sitting here in the dew-sweet morning, with the air that caressed their faces at once crisp and mild, they were vastly content.

Robin looked up at him finally, a touch of anxiety in her eyes.

"Are you having fun, Layne?" she asked in a soft whisper.

Layne's eyes, meeting hers, were warm and tender.

"Never so much fun in all my life," he assured her sincerely.

"I'm glad — " Robin began. Then her voice rose to a squeak, as something struck at her line and almost jerked the pole out of her hand. "I've got a bite," she gasped.

"You have, indeed," Layne answered, and watched the turmoil of the water as the fish fought for his freedom, lashing and trying to run away. Layne put an arm about her to steady her, and at that moment the fish broke water.

For an instant that seemed to them an age, they saw a giant head, round and bullet-shaped, framed by enormous whiskers. Then it was gone, still lurching and fighting.

"It's Old Granddad!" Robin gasped. "Layne, I've got him!"

Once more the fish rose, breaking water, fighting. Suddenly, Robin's hands slackened, and Layne saw her face was white with distress beneath her healthy tan.

"Hang on, honey, or he'll get away. He's just ready to heave the hook out," Layne urged, and reached for the pole. But Robin threw it from her. "Robin, why did you do that? He'll get away."

"I want him to, Layne. If he can throw the hook out of his mouth, he'll be all right, won't he? He'll live?"

"I suppose it isn't the first time he's been hooked and gotten away," Layne agreed. "He's a monster, and he must be very old. But you've talked about catching him for ages; you've wanted to. Why did you let him go?"

Robin looked up at him. He saw she was crying, and he cradled her in his arms.

"Why, Robin, honey, you deliberately let him get away, and now you're crying."

"I don't know why, Layne, honestly I don't." She wept, her face hidden against his shoulder, her small body shaking. "I've always dreamed of catching Old Granddad and boasting about it. And then when I had him, suddenly it seemed a terrible thing to do to anything as brave and valiant as he is. Here he's been living in his pool all these years, minding his own business and bothering nobody, and

242

then I come along and drag him out on the ground and let him die, just so I can boast I'm a good fisherman! That's pretty rotten, isn't it, Layne?"

"You silly little goof!" Layne held her and patted her back gently as though she had been a baby he was trying to 'burp.'

"I know," she said forlornly. "I *am* a fool — and I suppose you despise me. I couldn't help it, Layne. I couldn't kill him — I just couldn't."

She looked up at him, her face childishly tear-streaked, her eyelashes stuck together in little points, her eyes pleading with him to understand. And suddenly Layne bent his head and kissed her, a kiss that startled him almost as much as it startled her.

She drew away from his arms that were reluctant to let her go, and stared at him, wide-eyed, incredulous.

"You kissed me," she stated as though she could not believe it.

Layne's brows were drawn together in a puzzled scowl.

"Why, yes, I did, didn't I?" he admitted his own astonishment.

Robin's young face was scarlet now, and her eyes fell away from his.

"Well, don't worry about it, Layne," she told him. "We'll just forget it happened." She turned away.

Layne's arms reached for her and caught her, drawing her back to him. As he bent above her, his eyes searched hers with a pleading expression that made her heart leap like a suddenly spurred horse.

"Oh, no, we won't forget it," he told her sharply. "That is, you may — "

"I couldn't, ever, Layne," she cut in simply, meeting his eyes. "You see, I wanted you to. I've wondered and wondered what it would be like for you to kiss me. And it was even more beautiful than I could imagine."

"You precious little — " Layne's voice broke off, and he drew a long hard breath. "Look here, Robin, you *do* realize, don't you, that I'm old enough to be your father!"

244

"Why, what an awful whopper! I'm nineteen!" she flashed.

"And I'll be thirty my next birthday."

"So what?"

"I'm much too old for you, darling."

"Darling!" she breathed, radiant and starry-eyed. "You called me darling!"

"Why not? I love you."

She caught her breath, and for a moment she was speechless.

Layne laughed softly, a laugh that was a caress, and drew her close and hard in his arms, resting his cheek against her tumbled curls.

"Would you marry me, Robin?" he asked huskily at last.

"Marry you? Oh, Layne, I'd *love* it!"

He looked down at her anxiously.

"You won't mind leaving your beloved mountains? I have to live in New York. Does that frighten you?"

"Frighten me? What a silly thing to ask! As if anywhere in the world with you wouldn't be my favorite place!" She gave him her soft, sweet mouth for his kiss.

"Let's go tell Kirke," she said eagerly, after savoring the exquisite ecstasy of the moment.

"He's not going to be very pleased, I'm afraid," Layne cautioned her. "After all, you're his favorite sister."

"And he's my favorite brother," Robin pointed out. "But you're my favorite person! Don't you worry about Kirke. I can handle him."

Layne was slightly awed at her complete assurance as she stooped to pick up the can of bait and sprinkled it over the pool, laughing as the water was roiled with fish rising to get this unexpected breakfast.

"See?" she mocked. "The lazy good-for-nothings — expecting somebody to cook and serve breakfast in bed for them."

She laughed up at Layne; and together, hand in hand, they went back through the woods and up to the log house.

Kirke was coming from the barn, a brimming pail of milk in his hand.

He set it down when he saw them, and there was something about their radiance that made him eye them sharply.

"Oh, Kirke, I caught Old Granddad," Robin caroled joyously.

"Where is he?" asked Kirke.

"Oh, I let him go," Robin answered. She slid her hand into Layne's and said boastfully, "I caught myself something a lot more wonderful than Old Granddad; I caught Layne! He wants to marry me."

Dark anger flowed into Kirke's face, and he took a step toward Layne and said, "Now see here, Meredith — "

Robin put herself between the two men and faced Kirke.

"And don't you try to talk him out of it, either," she ordered hotly. "He loves me, and I adore him, and he wants to marry me, and that's that!"

"Believe me, Kirke, I didn't plan it this way," Layne said quietly.

"Didn't you?" Kirke's jaw was set

and hard. "She's too young to get married."

"Oh, phooey!" snapped Robin. "You know as well as I do that most of the girls I went to school with in the valley are married; some of them have babies by the time they're nineteen! They consider me an old maid!"

"It will be a long engagement, Kirke, if you want it that way," said Layne quietly.

"It will not!" protested Robin sharply. "We're going to be married right away — before he leaves for New York. Think I'm going to take a chance on losing him?"

"That you couldn't do, Precious, no matter how long an engagement we had," Layne told her. And the look in his eyes as he put his arms about her and drew her close, as well as the tone of his voice, did much to allay Kirke's fears. "I'll take good care of her, Kirke — I swear it."

Kirke drew a deep, hard breath and held out his hand.

"I believe you will," he agreed. "All I ask is that you make her happy."

"That will be my lifework from now on," Layne promised, and meant it.

"Well, I guess that's that, then," said Kirke heavily, and picked up the pail of milk and went on to the house, leaving Layne and Robin to follow as they wished.

Julie was in the kitchen when they came in, looking much lovelier than when she had arrived a few days before — rested, and with a tinge of color in her cheeks. She wore a pair of Robin's blue jeans and a thin shirt, and her shining, soft blonde hair was drawn back from her face into a pony-tail. She was cooking breakfast, and Robin gave a little shocked cry.

"Oh, Julie, you shouldn't be doing that," she protested.

"Why not?" asked Julie. "I'm not such a bad cook as all that."

She looked at them carelessly, smiling, and then her smile faded and her brows went up.

"What happened to you two? You look as if you'd met a pair of leprechauns who'd given you their pot of gold," she accused them.

"Oh, it's much more wonderful than that," Robin laughed excitedly. "Layne's discovered that he's in love with me, and we're going to be married."

"What?" gasped Julie. She met Layne's eyes and said before she could check the words, "Why, Layne, I thought you and Brooke — I mean — "

Stricken, Robin turned on Layne.

"Is that true? Are you in love with Brooke?" she asked, her voice shaking with the shock of the thought.

Layne put an arm about her and drew her close, looking down at her, his heart in his eyes.

"You silly little goof, I'm in love with you — head over heels in love with you," he told her, and there was comfort and reassurance in his voice. "I once thought that I was in love with Brooke, but I know now I was very much mistaken."

"I congratulate you, Layne, on discovering that in time," said Julie, and added warmly, "I congratulate you both with all my heart, and wish you all the happiness you both deserve. And nobody could possibly have any more than that."

Kirke came in from the back porch, where he had strained the morning's milk into a big brown crock, placed in a cool corner so the cream could rise.

"I take it they've told you the news," said Kirke mildly, and grinned at Robin. "Seems she caught Old Granddad this morning and then let him go."

"I also caught Layne," said Robin, her voice faintly husky. "And I'm not going to let him go — not for all the Brooke Hildreths in the world."

Kirke stiffened, and his eyes went from her to Layne.

"What's Brooke Hildreth got to do with this? You were not engaged to her, were you, Meredith?" he demanded sharply.

"Of course not," Layne answered as sharply. "We've always been good friends; I once thought I'd like to marry her. Then she met David — and that was that."

"Yes," said Julie softly, and there was a mist of tears in her eyes. "She met David, and that was that."

For a moment there was a taut silence, and then Julie straightened, smiled unconvincingly at them and said with a specious briskness, "Well, shall we have breakfast? It's all ready. I'm sure it's not as good as Robin could have prepared, but if we're all hungry enough — and I am, for one — it will be enough to keep body and soul together."

17

LATER in the morning, Robin came down to the barn where Kirke was working and leaned on the railing of the chicken house, where he was preparing a run for the new baby chicks that would hatch in a few days.

"Kirke, are you terribly busy?" she asked, and Kirke, who hadn't known she was there, looked up at her sharply.

"What's on your mind, Small Fry?"

"I'd like to ride over to Peacock Hill and see Brooke." Kirke straightened, and his jaw set hard.

"Why?"

Robin's eyes met his miserably.

"Because, Kirke, I have to know about her and Layne."

Kirke came to her and put his arm about her.

"That's a rotten way to start off

an engagement, honey — doubting Layne."

"Oh, I don't doubt Layne," she protested. "It's myself I'm worried about."

"I don't get it."

"It's just that — well, this morning, I sort of threw myself at Layne," she confessed miserably. "I was making a fool of myself about nearly catching Old Granddad, and Layne tried to comfort me, and the first thing I knew, he had kissed me, and I kissed him back, and then we were sort of engaged. He couldn't help himself, I suppose. I took an unfair advantage of him, in a way. So don't you see, Kirke, I have to find out for sure about him and Brooke."

"The thought of you taking advantage of a knowledgeable guy like Layne Meredith I find very funny."

"Don't laugh at me, Kirke — please don't!"

His arm tightened about her, and he gave her a slight shake.

"Now who in blazes is laughing, unless it's to keep from crying?" he demanded. "You haven't got a thing to worry about, believe me."

"Brooke's his kind of girl, and I don't know if I am or not," Robin went on doggedly. "She's very beautiful, and she knows about all the things that he knows, and I'm just a nothing — a nobody. How can I be *sure* it's me and not Brooke unless I talk to her — tell her about us?"

"And you think by her reaction to the news, you'll know?" he asked curiously.

As though puzzled by his density, she answered, "Well, of course — any woman would. Can we go?"

"Of course we can, Small Fry," Kirke answered. "Where is Layne? And Julie?"

"Julie's resting, and Layne's writing some letters. They won't miss us. We won't be gone long, because it won't take long for me to find out what I have to know."

Kirke nodded and led the way to the jeep, his eyes worried.

"Mind you," he said as he started the jeep, "I think you're worrying unnecessarily. No man could possibly choose Brooke Hildreth in preference to you — not unless he had a hole in his head you could drive the jeep through."

Robin looked up at him, puzzled.

"I thought you liked Brooke, Kirke."

"I did."

"Oh, something happened?"

"You might put it that way," Kirke agreed grimly. And she knew him so well that she realized it would be futile to try to question him.

Brooke and Elijah were working in the garden, putting out some plants from the greenhouse. Brooke wore battered jeans, with dirt on the knees where she had been kneeling in the soft, loamy earth. Her hair was pushed back of her ears, and there was a smudge on her forehead where her hand had pushed impatiently at the lock that kept falling over her forehead.

She sat back on her heels at the sound of the car, and when she recognized the jeep, she scrambled to her feet and came eagerly to meet them. Robin saw how her eyes went to Kirke and lingered and then fell away from the cold bleakness in his.

"Well, hello, strangers," Brooke greeted them gaily. "To what do we owe the honor of this unexpected pleasure, if I may coin a phrase?"

Unsmiling, Robin said, "Brooke, could I talk to you a minute — privately?"

Brooke stared at her and then at Kirke.

"Why, what ails the child?" she asked, smiling uncertainly.

"She has something on her mind," Kirke answered, unsmiling. "I'll have a word with Lije, while you two make with the chatter."

Brooke turned to watch him as he strode away, and when she turned back to Robin, there was a look in her eyes that Robin was too confused to be able to recognize or analyze.

"Well, what's it all about, Robin honey?" Brooke asked, as she stood beside the jeep where Robin still sat.

"I have to ask you a question, Brooke, and you have to promise me you'll tell me the truth — the whole truth."

Puzzled by the girl's solemnity, Brooke said quietly, "If I answer at all, Robin, it will be the whole truth. What is the question?"

Robin drew a deep, hard breath, clenched her small fists tightly and asked, "Brooke, are you in love with Layne?"

"I in love with Layne? Why, Robin, you absurd child, of course not."

There was such surprised sincerity, such obvious honesty in Brooke's startled negative, that some of the tightness left Robin's heart and her eyes brightened.

"Not even a little bit?" she insisted.

"Not even a little bit," Brooke answered. "He's my very best friend and I'm very fond of him. But he's always been more like an older brother, someone I could turn to for advice and comfort, when the going got rough."

"Julie said this morning she thought you and he — "

"Julie? Is she still here? I thought she was only staying overnight."

"She's been very ill, and she was so worn out by her trip down that Kirke suggested she stay on for a while and build up her strength."

"Oh, Kirke suggested it, did he?" There was an odd note in Brooke's voice, and her expression had stiffened.

"Oh, it was all of us, really." Robin was so intent on her own problems that she was quite unaware of Brooke's tone or her expression. "Layne thought it would be good for her to rest here awhile, and Kirke and I were delighted. She's doing fine. She loves it down here and says she doesn't mind if she never sees New York again."

"Oh, she does, does she?"

"You see, Brooke, Layne thinks he

wants to marry me!" Robin blurted out.

"Layne wants to marry you?" Brooke repeated, astounded.

Color poured into Robin's young face, and her chin went up.

"I know. It sounds crazy, doesn't it? Me, a nobody from the backwoods, and a man like Layne — "

"Will you be quiet?" Brooke cut in sharply. "You crazy little idiot! Layne is the luckiest man in the world if you love him."

"I do. Oh, Brooke, I just about worship him! I've never known anybody I could love before. But I thought if he was in love with you or you with him, he'd be a fool to marry me — if there was any chance he might marry you."

"Well, you can just dig a nice deep hole and bury that thought, because it's as dead as last year's leaves," Brooke told her vigorously. "I'm very fond of Layne, but marry him? Not in a million years!"

"You really mean that? You're not just mad at him and being spiteful?"

"I resent that crack," Brooke told her, more than half in earnest. "I'm not mad at Layne. How could I be? I told you — he's my best friend."

Robin drew a breath that seemed to come from the very heels of her scuffed shoes, and her young face bloomed into radiant beauty.

"Oh, Brooke! Thank you."

"Robin, you are a darling, but you're more than a bit of an idiot, too. Don't you realize how lucky Layne is, to be marrying you?"

That obviously was a thought that Robin found too fantastic to believe.

"Layne is lucky? Oh, Brooke, you've got it all wrong. I'm the one that's lucky. I never dreamed anybody like Layne could possibly want to marry *me*!"

"Now, you stop being so humble, infant! You're young, radiantly lovely, and sweet and decent and honest and straightforward. What man could possibly want a wife who was any more?"

"Brooke, you're sweet."

Robin blinked, above a tremulous smile, and called to Kirke, who spoke to Elijah, leaving the old man laughing as he came over to the jeep.

"The affairs of the world all settled?" Kirke asked politely, brushing Brooke with his cool gaze.

"All settled," Brooke answered as coolly, "except that I want you all to come to dinner tomorrow night. I'd say tonight, except that Miss Bessie would never forgive me if I didn't give her twenty-four hours' warning."

"Thanks, but I'm afraid I'm fresh out of 'soup-and-fish' clothes," Kirke answered before Robin could accept the invitation.

Brooke said quietly, "Come just as you are, Kirke, and you'll be most welcome."

"Oh course we'll come, Brooke; we'd love it," Robin tried to make anxious amends for Kirke's rudeness.

"Then I can count on you?" Brooke's question was addressed to Kirke. "You needn't dress."

"Oh, I'll wear my store-bought suit — I do have one, you know — and put slickum on my hair and we'll be here," Kirke answered dryly.

"I'm sure you'll look very handsome, and I'll look forward to seeing the store-bought suit," Brooke told his stiffly. "Seven o'clock?"

"Seven o'clock it is," Kirke answered, and started the jeep.

Brooke stood watching as the little car slid down the drive and vanished. She stood for a long moment, and then, her shoulders drooping, she went to give Miss Bessie the news that tomorrow night there would be four guests for dinner.

18

EZRA and Tom were delighted at the prospect of guests for dinner. And when, the following evening, Layne's car came up the drive, with the four guests, Brooke went to the door to meet them and brought them back to the drawing room where the two old men waited.

Robin was lovely in a simple yellow organdie frock, and Julie looked, as always, slimly elegant in a black satin sheath with a stole of black chiffon, star-sprinkled, about her thin shoulders.

Layne wore evening attire, and Kirke looked, to Brooke's eyes anyway, ruggedly handsome in a dark suit, a white shirt, dark tie and shoes. He would have looked, Brooke told herself as she performed her duties as hostess, perfectly at ease in even the most distinguished of the homes where she herself had always been an honored and welcome guest.

Miss Bessie had really outdone herself with the dinner, and was flushed and happy at the praise that came to her. Elijah, in an immaculate starched white coat, served with a composed deftness that made Brooke smile warmly at him as he bent over her, offering Hollandaise sauce for the broccoli. And, imperceptibly to all save herself, Elijah gave her the tiniest possible wink.

Julie was being her most charming to Ezra, who was obviously delighted with her. Kirke, who sat across from her, scarcely seemed to take his eyes off her, Brooke could not help noting.

Layne and Robin, one on either side of Tom, were hanging with frank fascination on some tale Tom was telling them about a research project on which he and Ezra had worked in Tuscany when they were younger.

After dinner, Brooke poured coffee in the drawing room, as usual. Then, her duties done, she glanced about the room. Layne and Robin were side by side on a big settee, their heads very close together, coffee cooling in the delicate china cups. Ezra and Tom were deep in conversation with Julie, who was either fascinated by them or else the world's best listener. But where was Kirke?

Brooke got up unobtrusively, since no one seemed to be paying any attention to her, and moved out of the room. The big front door stood open to the cool spring night, and she walked through it out to the terrace.

At the far end, above the drive, she saw the small fire of a cigarette glowing in the dark, and as though drawn against her will, she walked toward it.

Kirke turned as she came toward him, a glimmer that was ghostly in the darkness, her long white chiffon gown stirring about her feet, her face a pale oval above the glimmer.

Kirke tossed away his cigarette and

straightened as she approached him, waiting for her to speak.

"I don't dare to ask if you are having fun," she said evenly. "If you were, you wouldn't be out here alone."

"Oh, I don't know. After all, I'm a mountain man, and we're pretty solitary creatures," he drawled. "It was pretty warm in there."

"I know," Brooke agreed, and leaned against the low stone wall of the terrace, fingering a spray of climbing roses that was just bursting into bloom. "It's warm out here tonight. I suppose that means it's almost summer-time."

It was an inane thing to say; where were all her powers of sparkling conversation that had once made her so popular? All she could do now was stand there and chatter like a silly child.

"Nice of you to give this party," offered Kirke, obviously as much at a loss for sparkling conversational matter as she. "Robin scarcely slept last night, she was so excited about it."

"I'm so glad for her happiness," Brooke told him quietly. "Layne is really in luck. You won't be terribly lonely when she's married and gone?"

"Of course, but then I always knew I would be. I want her to be happy, and I believe Layne will make her happy."

"You must have some plans of your own, I'm sure."

"Plans?" he repeated as though unable to understand what she meant. "I have no immediate plans, except to go on living as I do now, here in the mountains."

She was very still for a long moment, and then she said huskily, "The mountains seem to be agreeing with Julie. She was never lovelier."

In the darkness, she could only guess at his expression. Beyond the terrace, away from the newly leaved trees, the moonlight was a pale silvery glimmer on the close-cropped lawn, and the air was crisp and fresh.

"Yes, she's a lovely girl," Kirke agreed, his tone without expression.

"She told me that you had agreed not to contest the will. It was decent of you."

Brooke's laugh was thin, unconvincing.

"Don't give me too much credit for that," she mocked him tautly. "She convinced me that if I tried it, she would destroy the will."

"I see," said Kirke.

"I'm sure you do." Her tone still held mockery, though she was trying very hard to keep it steady. "So you see it's Julie who was decent, not me. I'm not a very likable character, I'm afraid."

"Oh, I wouldn't say that." Kirke's tone held as much mockery as hers, and strain as she would to hear a touch of warmth in it, there was no warmth there.

"Wouldn't you? I felt sure you would be very happy to agree with me on that, judging from the things you said to me."

"May I take back those things?"

"Certainly not. Most of them were

true," Brooke assured him.

"I was unforgivably rude. I couldn't possibly understand and I had no right to judge you or your motives." Kirke was striving to ease the growing tension between them.

"Oh, I wouldn't say that," she repeated his own words.

There was a brief silence, and then Kirke said, "I suppose you'll be leaving Peacock Hill soon. You probably have plans."

"Oh, I do, but not for leaving Peacock Hill," she told him. "Elijah and I are going to raise peacocks. He likes the idea and thinks I should have a — well, I suppose he feels it would be a sort of hobby."

She felt the start with which he turned to face her, even though in the darkness they were scarcely visible to each other.

"You're staying on here?" he asked as though he could not believe it. "But won't it be terribly lonely for you? Won't you be bored?"

"That's what the peacocks are for, to keep me too busy to be lonely," she drawled. "And Miss Bessie says it's 'a sin and a shame for folks to let themselves be bored when the good Lord has filled the world with so much to do and so much to see.' And I think she's right, don't you?"

"No doubt." His tone was curt, and still touched with the amazement he felt at her decision to stay.

"This is the only home I've ever had," she said quietly. "I've never had a family, never belonged anywhere. And Uncle Ezra is a darling. He seems to like having me here. In a way, I feel that maybe they need me, though I realize that's pretty presumptuous of me. With Miss Bessie and Elijah here to take care of him, and Mr. Tom, they're snug as two bugs in a rug; but they *do* seem to like having me here. The moment I feel they don't, I'll leave, of course."

"Somehow I can't imagine you staying here," Kirke admitted slowly.

"Can't you? Why?"

"Oh, I'd think you'd want night clubs, theatres, concerts, fine shops."

"I've had all those ever since I was born, and I never knew any real happiness until I came here," she told him quietly, steadily. "Does that seem very strange to you? Julie's out of my own world, and she likes it here. Why shouldn't I?"

"Julie's been ill and is convalescing," Kirke pointed out. "I doubt very much she will be contented here for more than another week or so."

"Then she'll leave — and you'll go with her, of course."

There was a moment of stunned silence in which Kirke grappled with the utterly incredible thing she was suggesting.

"What in tarnation are you talking about?" he demanded when he could get his breath back.

"I saw the way you looked at her at dinner," said Brooke quietly. "It was the way David used to look at her. I

272

was too stupid then to realize what it meant until the whole world fell in on top of me. But I'm smarter now, and so I understand."

His voice, when he spoke, held an angry heat.

"Then I'd appreciate it if you'd explain so I can understand."

"She's in love with you."

"What? You're out of your mind!"

"And she's very lovely, and she would be delighted, I'm sure, if you'd ask her to marry you."

"I never heard such utter nonsense, such crazy talk, in all my life! All this talk about marriage — Layne and Robin started it — and it seems as if everybody else is trying to prolong it to utter absurdity."

"Do you mean you're not in love with Julie?"

"I am not," he managed at last in a choked, angry voice that struggled for calmness, "in love with Julie; I haven't the remotest intention of ever being in love with Julie. She'd laugh in my face — me, a clodhopper from the backwoods."

"Don't you dare call yourself that!" Brooke's sharp, angry tone startled him to silence. "Any woman in her right mind would be tickled to death to have you in love with her — any woman anywhere in the world would jump at the chance to marry you! You're wonderful."

Her voice shook itself to silence against the tears that clogged her throat, and she turned blindly to go back to the house. But Kirke's hand shot out and caught her arm and drew her back to him.

"Is that true, Brooke?" he asked her huskily. "Would any woman jump at the chance to marry me?"

"Of course."

"Would *you*, Brooke?"

He was holding her now, his hands on her arms, trying to pierce the darkness between them that showed him her face only as a pale oval, so that he had to guess at her expression. But when she spoke, he knew by the sound of her voice that she was crying.

"Oh, Kirke, *would* I?" she whispered.

"My darling," said Kirke, and his voice was little more than a whisper, shaken with a yearning tenderness that was like gentle fingers curling about her heart. "Oh, Brooke, I can't ask you — I don't dare."

"Because you know I'd say 'yes'?"

"Because I can't believe you could be happy here with me."

"I could be happy anywhere with you, Kirke — I love you so!"

He drew her gently into his arms and held her, cradling her, bending his head to take the kiss her soft mouth offered so eagerly.

After an interval that might have been no more than a moment but that to both of them was an age of ecstasy, he raised his head, and she knew from his tone that he was scowling, puzzled, uneasy.

"Look, honey, this is crazy," he told her huskily. "This is the only life I want, down here. I knew when I was away overseas that if ever I got back here, I'd never be willing to leave again. You must know that, darling; I couldn't leave here and go live your life, in your world — "

"I wouldn't ask you to, Kirke, my dearest — I promise that!"

"We marry for keeps down here, darling."

"That's the way I want it, Kirke — for keeps."

"It will be strange for you, maybe hard, dull — "

She pulled herself a little away from him, though her hands still clung to his arms.

"Are you trying to talk me out of it, Kirke?" she asked tautly. "Because if you are, you are wasting your time. You don't have to marry me if you don't want to; I won't try to make you. But you'll never get me to give up the conviction that being your wife would be the most perfect thing that ever happened to me. Everything else that has been before would be just nothing. But if you would rather not burden yourself with a wife who can't really be much help to you, but who'd try very hard to learn to do everything Robin's done for you — oh, Kirke, I'd try so very hard to be a good wife — your kind of wife."

Once more the tears choked her, and once more Kirke drew her into his arms and held her with the exquisite, ineffable tenderness of a man so deeply in love that he fears his lightest touch may bruise the beloved creature in his arms.

"Don't, darling, don't cry," he begged her, and kissed the tears that slid down her face. "You must take time and think about it. Maybe you'll decide it's too big a risk, giving up everything you've ever known to settle down here in the mountains. Take all the time you need to think about it; talk it over with Mr. Ezra, with anybody you like. If you decide you'd rather not, then I'll understand. But once you are married to me, then it'll be for always. I'll never let you go."

"That's the way I want it, darling — for always!" she told him softly, and framed his face, lean and brown and rugged, between her soft palms, and laid her cheek against his. "I don't need to think about it; I don't need to talk it over with anybody. I just need to know that you love me and want me and that it's for always!"

Behind them, though neither of them was aware of it, Robin and Layne appeared in the doorway. But whatever they had been about to say died unspoken, as they saw the two figures at the far end of the terrace, outlined against the moonlight beyond, melt into one shadow.

Layne drew Robin back into the big reception hall; his brows were drawn together in a frown of complete amazement.

"Well, what do you know?" he murmured softly.

Robin gurgled happily. "It's catching

— didn't you know?"

Layne looked at her, puzzled. "What's catching?"

"Love," she told him. "Didn't you know Kirke was crazy about Brooke, and that she liked him a whole lot? Well, I did!"

Layne grinned at her lovingly.

"Smart little gal, aren't you?" he teased her.

"Smart enough to see what's going on right under my nose," she boasted.

She looked up at him, and the laughter died in her eyes and was replaced by a starry radiance that touched Layne deeply.

"But I wasn't smart enough to think for even a minute that you were going to fall in love with me," she admitted soberly.

"Now that's a funny thing," Layne admitted with an honesty that rather startled her. "I didn't suspect a thing until you started crying about Old Granddad and I tried to comfort you by putting my arms around you; and

279

then I suddenly realized that that's what I wanted for the rest of my life — to hold you in my arms."

Robin nodded soberly.

"I knew you were surprised when I kissed you," she began.

"Hi, wait a minute — I kissed you first!"

"And I kissed you back, and suddenly there it was. We were in love! All of a sudden like — oh, like a flash of summer lightning!"

"That's a good description of it," he agreed. "You can know somebody for years and gradually get fond of her and think you could make a good marriage; and then some cute, sassy little gal comes along with a turned up nose and a tousled mop of curls, and — *boom*! You're in over your head. And you know that for you there couldn't be anybody else in all the world you'd want to marry!"

"And then, too," Robin apparently was following a train of thought all her own, "we have all the rest of our lives in which to get really acquainted!"

Layne laughed and caught her close and looked down into her eyes. "You're the most enchanting, unpredictable little creature I've ever met!"

She asked anxiously, "Is that good?"

"Honey, it's perfect! There'll never be any danger of our marriage becoming a bore, I promise you, because I'll never have the faintest idea what you'll do, or say next," he assured her frankly.

"I just hope I won't do or say anything that will embarrass you in front of your fancy friends," she confessed a secret fear.

"My fancy friends? Look, honey, I'm not a Park Avenue swell like Julie and Brooke. I'm a hard-working 'leg man' in a big law firm, and it will be years before we'll do any entertaining of the sort you're thinking about," he told her frankly.

"I'm glad," said Robin. "That will give me time to study up on etiquette and stuff. And meanwhile we can just have fun! Oh, Layne, I'm so happy I could fly!"

"So am I, darling, and isn't it swell?"

Layne held her close and kissed her hard. No other answer was expected or desired.

THE END